VOYAGE TO THE PLANETS

By
Richard Bliss, Ed.D.
Donald DeYoung, Ph.D.

Technical Advisor:
Danny Faulkner, Ph.D., Astronomy

Voyage to the Planets

First Edition 1994

Second Printing 1997

Library of Congress Catalog Card #94-092189
ISBN 0-932766-32-3

Institute for Creation Research
P.O. Box 2667
El Cajon, CA 92021

Cataloging in Publication Data
Bliss, Richard Burt
DeYoung, Donald B.
Voyage to the Planets

Printed in the United States of America

ACKNOWLEDGMENTS

Donald DeYoung

Richard Bliss

Our deep appreciation goes out to home-school parents and Christian school teachers who encouraged us to begin a *Voyage* series in science for their children. Our thanks also goes to those who gave their time to comment on the first drafts.

A book such as this, with its technical implications, could never be written properly without consulting science specialists. In this respect, we give our sincere appreciation to our colleagues and friends here at the Institute for Creation Research.

Each person has taken time from a very busy schedule to review this manuscript. Because of these dedicated professionals, we have a book about the planets which gives glory to the Creator of the heavens and the earth.

We need to identify one very important individual in the preparation of this book. Although the approach was new to many of us, we have ventured into a new style and dialogue approach among the characters in this book for the interest of our readers and thus for the better enjoyment and enhancement of their study. Our thanks goes to Marjorie Appelquist for the creative ideas that helped the manuscript flow in this new format.

In addition, our appreciation goes to personal friends who trusted us to complete this book. It is these friends to whom we give the credit for creating the seed moneys that will perpetuate the *Voyage* series for years to come.

Sincerely,

Richard B. Bliss, Ed.D.
Donald B. DeYoung, Ph.D.

Cover
Ramona Jeske

Technical Illustrations
Marvin Ross, Ramona Jeske, Wayne Spencer

Character Illustrations
Terry Walderhaug, Ramona Jeske

FOREWORD

Voyage to the Planets is the second in a series of books designed for high-school students. The purpose of the series is to present creation-science-content material in astronomy within a format that will be interesting for young people to read. In order to accomplish this, a fictional voyage into planetary space was devised. Two young high-school students, Ann and Jonathan, are key figures in the voyages, and their science activities exemplify the meaning of the scientific method. The experiences of Ann and Jonathan provide the basis for scientific questions and answers in the text. Their leader, a navy officer called Captain Venture, has talents that cover the whole spectrum of science. He is the model of scientific thinking. Whatever questions Ann and Jonathan can't answer through their own library research, the captain is sure to have an answer for.

The main objective of this voyage is to bring current planetary science observations into focus and fix them on the creation-science issue. In fact, one of the charges to the team is to look for evidence of God's handiwork in creation on the voyage.

In order to accomplish this, our team of science explorers becomes involved in futuristic travel activities. The reader will find, in this story, that space-shuttle technology is advanced to "Star Trek" proportions. Rapid transportation and lander technology well beyond the state of current scientific knowledge is assumed. The facts of astronomy, however, are clearly followed; never fantasized.

The purpose of *Voyage to the Planets* is to deliver important creation-science concepts through an exciting fictional story line. This book is a sincere attempt to make young people aware of the serious failures of evolutionary thinking in astronomy. Even more important, *Voyage to the Planets* sends a clear message, through science, that the best model for explaining the origin of the planets is the creation model.

CONTENTS

OUR SPACE TEAM

Ann Jackson is a senior in high school from San Diego, California. She wants to go to medical school and would be interested in astro-medicine as a specialty when she becomes a doctor.

Jonathan Andrew is a senior in high school from Whitefish Bay, Wisconsin who has just won the national biophysics award. Jonathan wants to be an astronaut scientist.

Richard Brock is the 1st officer on board the space shuttle and was also a test pilot for the Northway Aviation Corporation. He has been an astronaut for the past five years with NASA, as well as being an experienced space traveler.

Major Steven Paul was a test pilot for several aeronautical firms before he came to NASA. He also has a degree in physics and chemistry from MIT.

Newton is named after the famous creation scientist, Isaac Newton. He appears from time to time in the pages of our book. Although he never interrupts Captain Venture, Ann, or Jonathan, he does give a more detailed understanding of scientific and sometimes Biblical points that are discussed by our adventurers.

INTRODUCTION AND PURPOSE

Our scientist, Captain Venture, is depicted as having a very distinguished background as a captain in the U.S. Navy. He is a scholar in every sense of the word and has a sophisticated background in many fields of science.

Voyage to the Planets shows the captain as an individual who has had a significant change in his thinking. Having been trained as an evolutionist in the university systems of the U.S., he now sees that the unbiased scientific evidence demands a creator. Captain Venture now believes that a Master Designer put the universe into place. Like many other scientists of his day, he was trained that only evolution could be scientific. Now, as a creation scientist, he believes in the historical truth of the origin of life described in Scripture. This change has given Captain Venture a new outlook toward science and the interpretation of scientific data, as well as a personal, daily walk with the Creator.

This book describes an exciting voyage on a space shuttle. Captain Venture and two specially selected student companions will be viewing the planets first hand—in a fictional sense—with the most current information and photographs from the National Aeronautics and Space Administration (NASA). This journey to the planets begins, as all journeys of this nature do, with a lot of ground-school and classroom time. A preview of the coming journey for the young astronauts is carefully rehearsed in their ground-school briefings. The reader will enjoy some of the quips and dialogue between Jonathan, Ann, and the captain as they run into new experiences in their exploration of the planets.

Voyage to the Planets is designed to make interesting reading in science, to present accurate information about the planets and our solar system, to be used as supplementary reading in science, and, above all, to glorify and acknowledge the magnitude and majesty of our Creator.

Chapter 1

OFF TO WHERE?

Our story begins as Jonathan and Ann return to the Air Force Planetarium. They had met Captain Venture for the first time on their previous shuttle trip when they studied the stars (see first book in this series). That was a frightening first-time experience for both of them. Now, after many hours of study and adventure with the captain, their knowledge and experience had helped them overcome their anxiety.

"Jonathan," commented Ann as they walked up the pathway, "I wonder if Captain Venture will tell us about the Hubble Space Telescope again."

"I hope not!" commented Jonathan. "You really pressed his story button the last time you brought that subject up."

"Well," said Ann in her own defense, "at least we'll remember what that telescope is like for a long time to come."

"Yes, we sure will," answered Jonathan. "That story was really interesting, wasn't it? We've only begun to see what the advantage of the Hubble is going to be to astronomers in the future."

"Well, I'm sure glad the captain knows so much about it," declared Ann.

"Me, too! I really am anxious for him to bring us up to date on what Hubble is doing," commented Jonathan.

At that moment Captain Venture came into view and started down the walk toward them. "I thought I'd come out to meet *you*, this time," he quipped, "but I'll have to be honest with you both. I was wondering if you'd be taking me up on this adventure after our faulty-telescope experiences on the last voyage."

"Why do you say that, Captain?" asked Jonathan, "Ann and I had an exciting time."

"In fact," added Ann, "we've been praying that you wouldn't change your mind."

The captain smiled. "Well, we'll try not to have any equipment failures this time," he replied.

The team seemed very happy to be together again, and they spent quite some time talking right there on the sidewalk.

Finally, Captain Venture said, "Well, tomorrow will be time enough to get started, so do everything you have to do today to get ready for our study sessions."

"I'm ready to get started right now," stated Jonathan eagerly.

"Me, too," added Ann.

"Not so fast!" laughed the captain. "Neither of you have even gotten yourselves settled into the dorms yet, so let's get started with first things first. I'll have an outline for our briefing that will start tomorrow at—you guessed it—0700 hours.

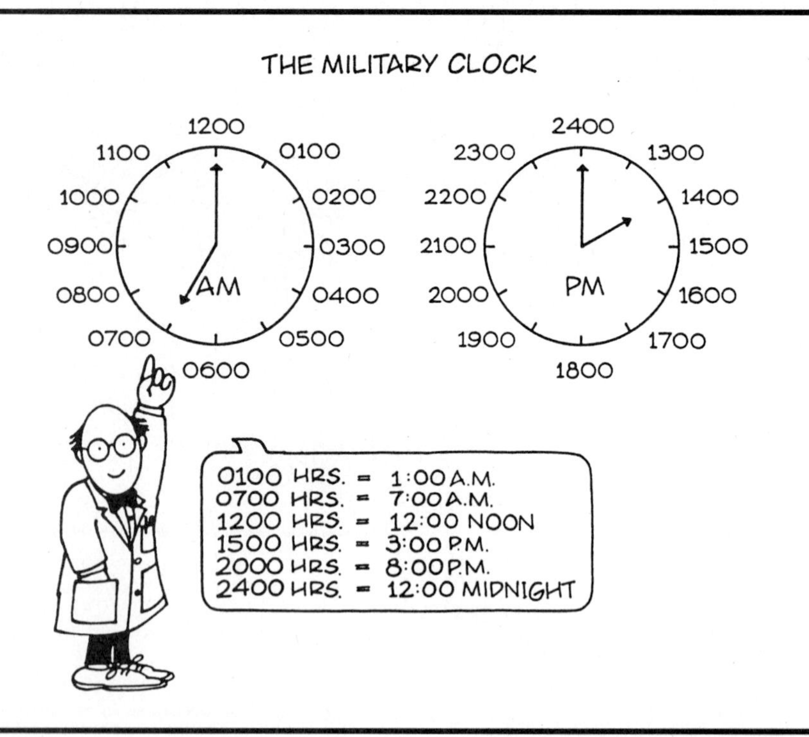

Ann and Jonathan groaned, and the captain laughed again. Zero seven hundred hours seemed very early to the young astronauts. They had slipped out of their early-morning routine since their last adventure with the captain, and getting up early wasn't going to be easy, but their excitement began to grow as they thought about their upcoming trip.

They both knew there would be something very special about this new adventure. The tone of voice and the secret nature of the mission made them realize that things were going to be quite different about this experience.

So finally, here they were again, sitting in the briefing room in the Air Force Academy planetarium. Somehow, this time, there was an air of uncertainty about the whole thing. They didn't know where this new adventure was going to lead.

Ann commented to Jonathan as they sat waiting, "Do you feel more nervous this time?"

"Yes, Ann," Jonathan shivered, "in some ways I do. I guess it's because of the secrecy of the mission. But remember, the last time, we knew what we would be doing from the very beginning. We knew that we would be studying the stars and constellations from the space shuttle platform. This time, we don't even know what our adventure is going to be about."

"We know for sure that NASA will be involved," said Ann, "so this means a space trip of some kind.

Just then Captain Venture walked into the room.

Ann leaned over to her friend: "You can set your watch, Jonathan —0700 hours—right on the dot!"

Jonathan nodded and grinned: "Now why did you have to say that? It makes me remember how sleepy I am."

"Good morning, Ann and Jonathan. I'm sure you're anxious to know what the big secret adventure is all about," stated the captain as he opened the meeting.

"Yes, Sir!" said Ann and Jonathan in unison.

"And why is this mission so secretive, Captain?" asked Jonathan.

"Well, I knew this would be something that would concern you, but I hope you aren't too worried. Let me explain that some of the new technology we'll be using on this adventure is known to only a very few top engineers. The U.S. government wants to keep some of these secrets quiet for awhile, so we're restricted from announcing about this project too openly," explained the captain.

"However, here's the big announcement you've been waiting for! This voyage is going to be a trip to the planets."

"To the planets!" the young people shouted. "Wow!"

"I can't believe it! This has always been my dream," Jonathan exclaimed, when the shock was beginning to wear off and he was finally able to speak again.

"No wonder this has been such a hush-hush project," spoke up Ann in surprise. "The rockets on our last trip would never have been able to achieve this goal."

The captain was pleased at their reaction and not at all surprised. "You're right, Ann, but there's even more to the story. We'll be the first humans ever to get beyond the moon. In fact, this will be the very first time that a shuttle spacecraft has ever orbited beyond the **Van Allen Radiation Belts**. Remember when we sent our astronauts to the moon? They didn't travel in a shuttle."

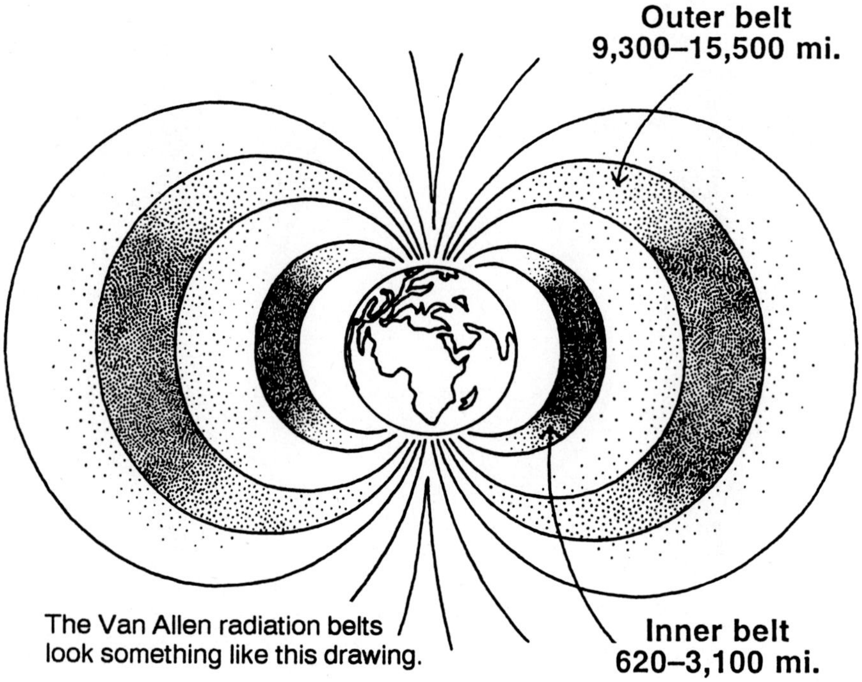

Outer belt
9,300–15,500 mi.

Inner belt
620–3,100 mi.

The Van Allen radiation belts look something like this drawing.

The Van Allen belts are regions surrounding the earth containing intense radiation and high-energy charged particles.

The captain continued: "The modifications needed for this project are beyond anything man has ever tried before. We'll be using modified engines and a very special fuel to make this trip. In fact, we'll be using an entirely new method of travel."

"It seems that man's intelligence has no limit when it comes to new ideas and discoveries in science," Jonathan commented.

"Jonathan!" Ann interrupted, "It was God's design of man's brain in the first place that gave him the intelligence to do this."

"You're right, Ann. Sorry about that! I didn't mean to imply that we could do it without God's help."

"Well," continued the captain, "the new method of travel is highly classified. I can tell you this, though—we'll be traveling at speeds that man has never traveled before. This, of course, is because of a very elaborate propulsion system."

"Will we be cleared to get this information?" asked Ann.

"You can be sure that you will know about all of those things that are important to do the job."

Both young people agreed that the answers probably would be so technical they wouldn't be able to understand them anyway.

There were other people in the room listening to Captain Venture teach the young people, and his next statement made the entire room a vacuum of quiet. "We'll be going to the planets with the express purpose of studying each of them from a **'scientific creation'** point of view."

"Just exactly what do you mean, Captain?" asked Ann.

"Well, Ann," the captain answered, "we'll be looking for scientific evidence that will point to intelligent design. In fact, we'll be looking for the handiwork of the Creator—for evidence of how God set the planetary laws in place—why the planets have such special characteristics and how the earth could have become such a perfect place for life. I could go on and on, but I'm sure you're getting my point."

"Can you elaborate on that a little more, Captain?" asked Jonathan.

The captain thought a moment. "I guess you could say that we'll be looking for evidence of **symmetry (orderliness)—purpose** and **interdependence**—one thing depending upon another. If we can find this kind of evidence, then we can be sure that an intelligent designer was the master-planner of this whole universe."

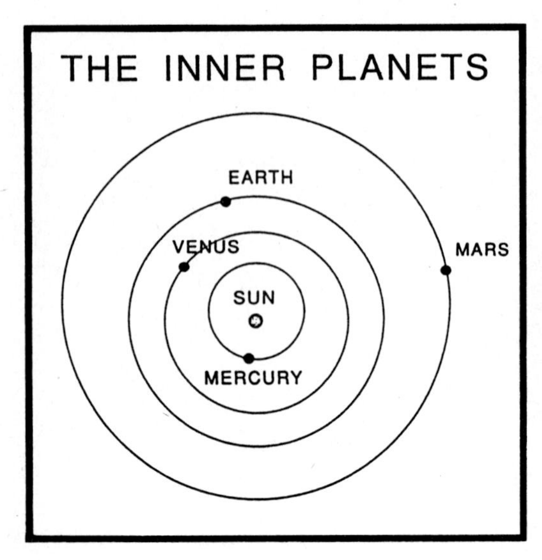

The captain paused a moment to let the statement sink in and then pulled down a wall screen that showed the nine known planets in our solar system. "I want to give you a quick review of the planets before we venture into their deep dark secrets. We'll be looking at each planet in depth a little later."

"The first four: Mercury, Venus, Earth, and Mars are called the **inner planets**. This is the group of smaller planets."

"When you say smaller, what is that related to?" asked Ann.

"Well, I see you remember our discussions about things being relative from the *Voyage to the Stars* expedition, Ann." The captain went on to explain that **size, mass, distance to the sun**, and **atmospheric pressure** of the planets are usually thought of in relation to the earth. The earth is considered to be a "one" on a number scale.

Planet Volumes
(Earth equals one)

MERCURY	0.06
VENUS	0.86
EARTH	1.00
MARS	0.15
JUPITER	1400.00
SATURN	833.00
URANUS	84.01
NEPTUNE	59.00
PLUTO	0.006

"This means that if the earth is 'one,' then, according to that chart, Mercury would be six hundredths of the volume of the earth. Is that right?" asked Jonathan.

"That's it exactly," responded the captain with a nod.

"Is this true of all planets?" asked Ann.

"Yes," responded the captain. "This includes all of them—even the giant planet, Jupiter."

"That would be 1,400 times the volume of the earth," figured Jonathan quickly.

"Very good! That's exactly right," responded the captain with a smile. "You're getting better and better at your figuring."

"Well, I'm pretty good at figuring, too," retorted Ann.

"Of course you are," the captain laughed, "and you'll have plenty of chances to prove it on the mission.

"But now to get back to the planets, the four larger planets, **Jupiter, Saturn, Uranus,** and **Neptune**, have a special name. They're called the **Jovian Planets**. They get their name from the Latin word for 'Jupiter.' They're also called the 'outer planets.'"

"It sounds like Pluto has been left out of that group," commented Ann.

"Well, I think we'll find out some very interesting things about that tiny planet also, but let's get on with this briefing session for now," prodded the captain.

He went on to explain that the voyage would be taking them close to the planets, and pointed out that it would be essential to know everything they could about the planets before they even started their journey. He indicated that many mistakes could end the mission and perhaps even their lives.

Ann and Jonathan were a little subdued by his comments. For the first time, they began to realize that this wouldn't be just a joy ride, but a serious adventure.

"You've given us a great challenge, Captain," spoke up Jonathan, "but if this means we can learn more about God's handiwork in creating the solar system, then I'm all for it."

"I think the danger adds a little more to the challenge, Captain, but I'm still ready to go," responded Ann.

"Captain, will we be traveling with the same flight crew as before?" asked Jonathan.

"Yes, we're very fortunate in this regard," answered the captain. "Major Steven Paul and Captain Richard Brock will be part of our flight crew."

"Great," said Jonathan and Ann in unison. "They were swell companions."

Captain Venture smiled. "Oh, there's something else I need to tell you. After our preliminary planetary training here at the Air Force Academy, we'll be sending you to Houston and Cape Canaveral for additional special training. You'll be going through their astronaut program."

"And that's the best place to get that training, isn't it, Captain?" asked Jonathan.

"It certainly is," he responded, "since the rigor of this voyage requires this special training."

"And it will certainly help that Jonathan and I have been to the advanced-training sessions at the U.S. Space Camp in Huntsville, Alabama," stated Ann.

NASA

"That's called the U.S. Space and Rocket Center," Jonathan corrected her.

"Okay, okay," responded Ann, "but I remember how exciting it was for us when we were high-school juniors. . . ."

"And how tough it was," groaned Jonathan.

The captain smiled as he listened to them talk about their experiences at the Space and Rocket Center.

"Well, let me just add this," interrupted the captain. "You've received some of the finest training there is in the U.S. for high-school kids. This training has helped you a great deal already, and I know you'll be interested in an extended part of your training at the different centers."

"Could we have an outline of what we'll be covering in the briefing sessions, Captain?" asked Jonathan.

"Yes," added Ann, "so we can review what we know of the planets and the laws they obey."

"Oh, you're way ahead of me," laughed the captain. "That's just exactly what we're going to do. We'll have to press our memory buttons in chemistry and physics so we can evaluate the planets and the

laws they obey, so get your notebooks out. This is what we'll be covering in these sessions. . . ."

"Hey, Ann, loan me a pen," Jonathan leaned over and whispered to Ann.

PROPERTY	SMALLEST	LARGEST
Rotation Period	Jupiter (10 hours)	Venus [retrograde] (243 days)
Revolution period	Mercury (88 days)	Pluto (248 years)
Speed	Pluto (10,600 mph)	Mercury (107,000 mph)
Specific Gravity	Saturn (0.7)	Earth (5.5)
Axis tilt	Venus, Jupiter (3°)	Uranus (98°)
Orbit eccentricity	Venus (.007)	Pluto (0.25)
Number of moons	Mercury-Venus (0)	Jupiter-Saturn (dozens)
Brightness	Pluto	Venus
Atmospheric Pressure	Mercury, Pluto	Venus (90 x Earth)
Temperature	Pluto (-390° F)	Venus (890° F)
Size	Pluto	Jupiter

"You mean you came to this briefing session and forgot your pen?" asked Ann incredulously!

"Shh!" begged Jonathan, "I know, I know, but I could hardly get dressed this morning, let alone remember all my supplies."

At that point the captain put an outline on the chalkboard. "We'll start here," he said, pointing to the board, "but not until tomorrow. I think we've had enough for one day. And, besides, I'm hungry," he grinned. "How about you?"

The young astronauts nodded eagerly.

"So, I'll see you tomorrow morning at 0700 hours," smiled the captain as they left.

Questions

1. Change the following to military times:
   9:00 a.m. ____________________
   12:00 noon ____________________
   6:30 p.m. ____________________
2. Change these military values to everyday time:
   0200 hours ____________________
   0650 hours ____________________
   1800 hours ____________________
3. Which planet is
   smallest? ____________________
   brightest? ____________________
   farthest in orbit? ____________________

Chapter 2

OUR CREATOR'S UNIVERSE

"I got a lot more out of my Bible devotions this morning," commented Ann to Jonathan on their way to the briefing room the next day.

"Oh, how come?" asked Jonathan.

"Well, I think it's because my brain was more awake than it was yesterday."

"Yes, I wasn't quite as sleepy this morning either," agreed Jonathan. "And that's a good thing for both of us, because we're sure going to need our wits about us today. This is when the captain said we're going to outline our objectives, so it's bound to be an exciting day, when we finally will have a clear understanding of what this adventure is going to be all about."

"I guess the only thing that's bothering me so far is about how we're going to travel so fast," said Ann with a frown.

"Well, why should that bother you?" asked Jonathan in a rather exalted manner.

"Well," answered Ann hesitantly, getting out a pen and a piece of paper from her notebook, "when you consider that the earth is one astronomical unit from the sun—that's 93 million miles, and Jupiter is 5.2 astronomical units from the sun—that's 483 million miles, how long do you think it's going to take us to get to even the planet Mercury, let alone Pluto, which averages 39.44 astronomical units from the sun, or almost 3667 million miles?"

This model shows one astronomical unit, the distance between the earth and the sun.

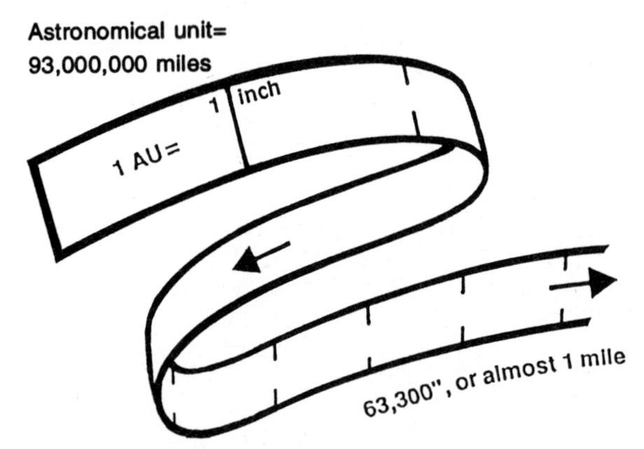

One light year is the distance light travels in a year at the speed of 186,000 miles per second.

"You know, Ann, I never thought of that. We'll have to ask Captain Venture to give us an explanation. Remember, though, that there are some things he can't reveal to us about our space shuttle, and maybe that's one of them."

Jonathan looked at his watch. "Hey," he almost shouted, "we'd better get going. We don't want to be late—that sure wouldn't go over very well with the captain."

They hurried up the walk and into the briefing room and were safely in their seats just before the captain arrived—exactly at 0700 hours.

"Good morning," said the captain with a grin. "Are you more awake this morning?"

At a nod and a responding grin from each of the young people, he went on. "Well, we have a lot to cover today, so let's get with it."

"Captain," Jonathan interrupted, "Ann and I were talking on the way over this morning. Something's bothering us."

"Go ahead," invited the captain, "out with it! Tell me what's bothering you and we'll try to resolve it right now."

"Well, we're wondering about the great distances we're going to be traveling. How can we get to all the planets with a spacecraft like the shuttle?"

"That's a good question," responded the captain. "I knew you'd be asking that question sooner or later.

Two inquisitive minds like your's and Ann's wouldn't pass that up for long. Since I've had a hunch you'd be asking about this sooner or later, I asked Major Paul and Captain Brock to stand by and answer some of your questions. At least they'll be able to answer those that aren't classified."

Both Jonathan and Ann stood up to greet Captain Brock and Major Paul when they came into the room, and then, when they were seated, Ann made the first comment:

"We know we're going to have a good voyage to the planets. Jonathan and I have been praying that both of you would be a part of the crew, so we're glad you're going with us."

"I understand we're going to have additional crew members for the flight deck," commented Jonathan.

"Yes, that's true," responded Captain Brock. "We have to carry extra crew members for trips such as this. There will be much to do."

Captain Brock added that they hadn't made a final decision as to who the new crew members would be, but that there were several in training with them.

"One thing I can assure you, though, is that this will be a new experience for them."

"Yes, and for us, too," added Jonathan.

Captain Venture directed his next comment to the two men. He told them about Jonathan's and Ann's question.

"Major Paul, I thought it would be best for you and Captain Brock to take the question relating to the propulsion system we'll be using. How much information can we give them without breaching security?"

"Because your security clearance does not require you to know the exact details, we will give you only general information about our propulsion system," said Major Paul.

"I can tell you this, however—we'll be traveling at tremendous speeds, as you can imagine, in order to get from one planet to another. These speeds will be called **warp speeds**. The reason for this term is because the speeds are so incredible. We'll be clicking off astronomical units in minutes.

"Fortunately, these speeds will have little effect upon the astronauts on this mission. This will be something for those of us on the flight deck to deal with in our navigation calculations."

"Thanks for explaining this," Jonathan interrupted, "but can you give us an idea about the shuttle craft that we'll be traveling in?"

Major Paul nodded for Captain Brock to answer this, and the captain continued: "The shuttle that we'll be traveling in will be modified internally. In spite of this, it will be almost identical to the spacecraft we used on our last voyage. I can assure you that you'll be traveling in familiar surroundings—at least inside the space shuttle."

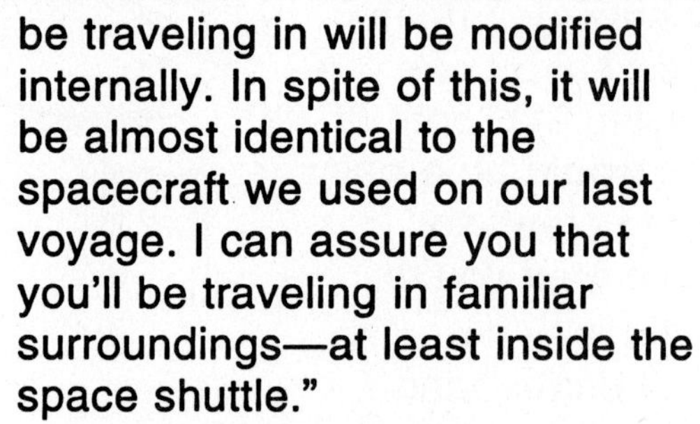

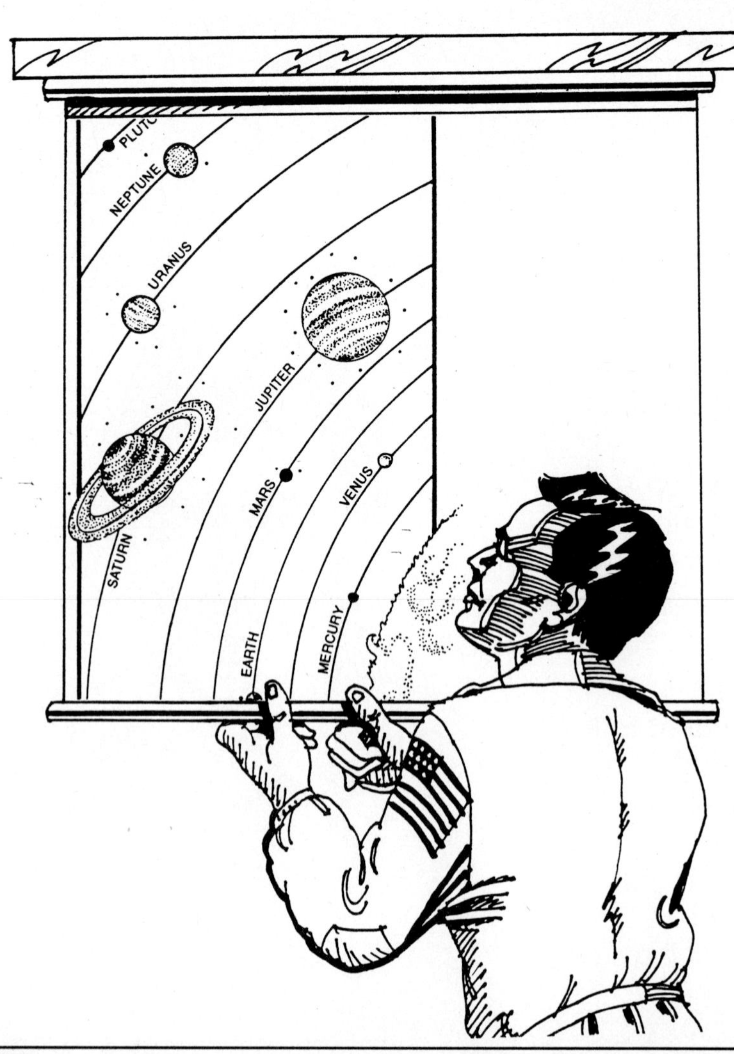

Captain Venture spoke up at this point: "Thanks for your input, Captain Brock and Major Paul. We'll be asking you back later, but for now, we have to get on with the astronomy briefing. Thanks again for coming in."

Both Ann and Jonathan again stood while their good friends left the room.

"I'm sure glad they'll be going with us again," commented Ann.

"Me, too," agreed Jonathan.

"Well," said the captain, "we've much to cover in our briefing today, so we'd better get on with it."

With that, the captain pulled down the chart of the planets

and got his pointer out. "We'll be talking about each of the planets later, but there are some general things we need to know about first."

"Are these general things that we can apply to all the planets?" asked Ann.

"Yes, Ann. For instance, we'll be talking about their speed and their distance from the sun."

"Captain Venture, what do these things have to do with the planets themselves?" asked Jonathan.

"That's a good question, Jonathan, and that's the reason for this briefing.

"In order to understand the planets, we have to understand where they are and hopefully why they are there." Captain Venture pointed to the chart. "We'll be talking in terms of **astronomical units**, or **AU's**, when we deal with the planets."

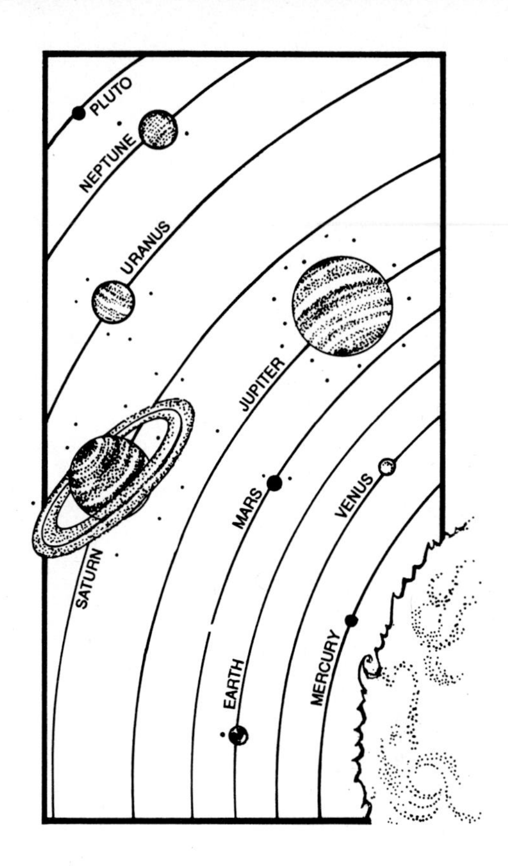

Mean (Average) Planet Distance From Sun in AU's*

MERCURY	0.39
VENUS	0.72
EARTH	1.0
MARS	1.52
JUPITER	5.20
SATURN	9.54
URANUS	19.19
NEPTUNE	30.06
PLUTO	39.53

* AU = 1 Astronomical unit = 93,000,000 miles.

"That's a lot different than the **light years** we were using when we learned about the stars on our last shuttle flight," commented Jonathan.

"Yes," added Ann.

"That's right," answered the captain. "Notice the **mean distances** of the planets on the chart," he said as he pointed to each one.

"But why do we always have to speak in terms of **mean**?" asked Ann. "What is the meaning of the word, 'mean,' anyway?"

The captain laughed. "It does seem to be a strange term," he went on to explain, "but when used in this way, it simply means a middle point between extremes, or a point that lies within a range of points. This is a statistical term."

"Don't we know exactly how far the planets are?"

"Yes, we know this at any moment in time, but these distances change as the planets travel in their orbits," the captain answered. "Remember, the planets don't orbit in a perfect circle around the sun. As a result, the distance from the planet to the sun changes as the planet travels in its orbit."

"In other words, to find a planet's mean distance from the sun, we average all of the distances of the many points that the planet passes through in its orbit. Isn't that it?" asked Ann.

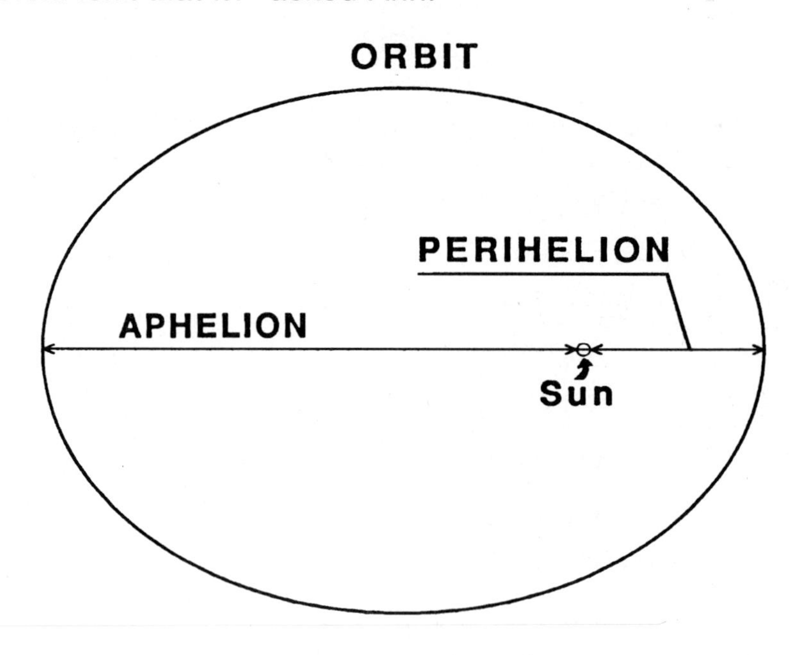

The orbit of a planet around the sun is called an ellipse, or flattened circle.

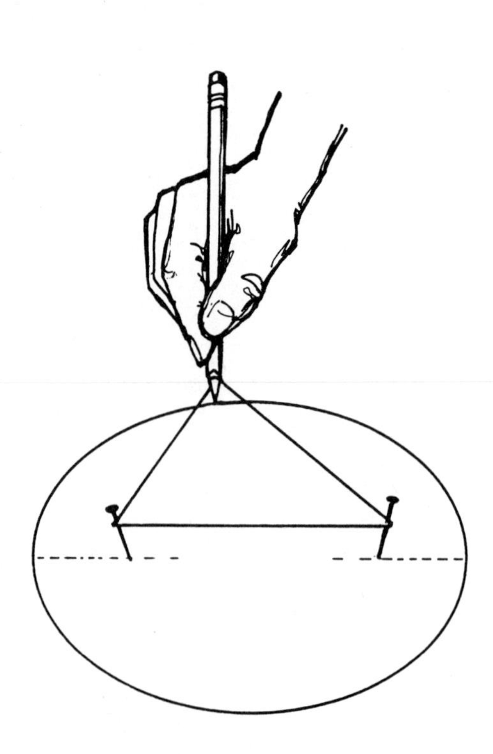

You can construct an ellipse—the path that planets travel around the sun. Place a sheet of paper on a thick cardboard backing and stick two pins or thumb tacks in the paper. Tie a string around the pins. With a pencil, draw a curved line on the paper as far as the string allows. The resulting egg-shaped curve is called an ellipse. You can construct other ellipses by varying the distance between the pins.

"Yes, that's a good way to put it, Ann," the captain responded. "Now let's talk about the importance of a planet's **period of revolution** around the sun." Pointing to the chart again, he asked Jonathan if he could see something special about the distances from the sun.

"Well, the numbers get larger as the planets get further away from the sun," observed Jonathan.

"But anyone can see that," Ann piped in.

"Well," said Jonathan hesitantly, "the earth is one astronomical unit. . . . Oh, I see it now! The earth and the sun are the basis for measuring the other distances." His face brightened as he realized he had figured it out.

"Good for you!" the captain responded. "You've got it!"

"And I thought you never would," Ann teased.

"That's just the point I wanted to make," said the captain. "Everything we know about the universe and the solar system starts from where you and I are sitting right here on the earth."

Ann brought up another subject about the planets that she wanted to ask the captain. "We hear so much about how long planets take to go around the sun. Would you explain that to us?"

"Sure," said the captain. "This is a very important factor in the solar system. We have nine planets traveling around the sun at different speeds."

Planet Revolution Times

PLANET	IN DAYS	IN YEARS
MERCURY	88	0.241
VENUS	224.7	0.615
EARTH	365.3	1.0
MARS	687	1.88
JUPITER	4,333	11.86
SATURN	10,759	29.46
URANUS	30,686	84.07
NEPTUNE	60,189	164.8
PLUTO	90,465	248

The captain turned to the charts again and pointed to the revolution speeds of each planet. "The period of revolution of a planet is the number of earth days that it takes for a planet to complete one full revolution around the sun. Look carefully at this chart.

"Now, can either of you see any special pattern in the revolution of the planets?"

"I can see one thing, for certain," said Ann. "The further the planets are away from the sun, the longer it takes them to go around the sun."

Planet's Speed Around Sun
(in kilometers per second)

MERCURY	47.8
VENUS	35.0
EARTH	29.8
MARS	24.1
JUPITER	13.1
SATURN	9.6
URANUS	6.8
NEPTUNE	5.4
PLUTO	4.7

"The big thing in my mind is how they got there in the first place," spoke up Jonathan. "It's easy to see the perfect order in the solar system, but how did it all get into place?"

Pointing to the chart again, the captain said, "We haven't even considered the tremendous speeds at which these planets are traveling in their revolution around the sun. Look at the chart, which shows the speeds at which the planets are traveling as they revolve around the sun."

He threw a challenge out to Jonathan and Ann: "Who wants to be first to talk about what our chart shows us?"

"The first obvious thing," Jonathan volunteered, "is what Ann just mentioned, that the farther the planets get from the sun, the slower their speed."

"A planet travels most rapidly when it is nearest the sun and most slowly when it is farthest from the sun. They are farther away and don't need the speed to keep gravity from pulling them into the sun, Captain," offered Ann.

"You're correct on that score, Ann," answered Captain Venture.

"I think I see a pattern starting to form here, Captain," remarked Jonathan. "It looks like there is an order and interconnection to all of the data we're observing. I don't know what it is yet, but I'm going to keep my eyes open."

"Don't worry, Jonathan," the captain reassured him, "none of us has all the answers yet, but each bit of scientific evidence brings us closer."

It was obvious that both Ann and Jonathan were getting even more enthused by the minute, and Ann commented that she thought this voyage was going to be even more exciting than their last one.

The captain noticed their growing enthusiasm and was pleased. "Well, we have more data about the planets to consider during this briefing."

After both young people had studied the charts briefly, Jonathan made the first comment: "I understand why the earth is used as a standard, but I'm not sure what I'm supposed to learn from these charts. What is the point, Captain?"

Mass of Planets vs. Their Diameter (Earth equals one)

PLANET	MASS	DIAMETER
MERCURY	0.056	0.038
VENUS	0.815	0.95
EARTH	1.0	1.0
MARS	0.107	0.53
JUPITER	317.9	11.2
SATURN	95.1	9.4
URANUS	14.5	4.0
NEPTUNE	17.2	3.9
PLUTO	0.002	0.2

"Well," answered the captain, "by using the earth as 'one,' we have a simple standard to follow. We can now use our own planet Earth for a standard. "We have a lot to look over. We want to see the handiwork of our Creator and report accurately about our observations, but we've had enough for today. Goodbye for now, and I'll see you bright and early at 0700 hours tomorrow."

"Well, early, anyway," Ann responded to Jonathan. "I'm not sure how bright we'll be."

On the way down the walk outside of the building, Ann commented again: "I want to pinch myself to see if I'm really here. Just think, Jonathan! We're going to be looking for **scientific evidence** that will testify to God's creative hand."

"I'm excited, too!" declared Jonathan, "and that's only part of it. There's no question about the truth of the *Bible's* account of creation; that's history! The question now is, how can we see God's handiwork from a *scientific* perspective!"

"We've got a lot of work to do for tomorrow, that's for sure," responded Ann. "I'll see you in the library after lunch this afternoon."

Questions

1. Explain what is meant by an elliptical orbit.
2. Explain what is meant by average distances.
3. Do all planets travel around the sun at the same speeds? Explain this.
4. Why did Jonathan think there had to be a creator for the planets?
5. Which planet has the greatest mass?
   the smallest diameter?
   the fastest revolving (orbit) time?

Chapter 3

PLANETS MERCURY AND VENUS

Breakfast time arrived early for Ann and Jonathan the next day. It seemed as though they had just gone to bed, and now it was time for them to start again.

"Hi, Jonathan," Ann exclaimed as she brought her breakfast tray over to the table. "How do you feel today about yesterday's briefing?"

"Well, I have to admit it gave me a whole lot to think about," commented Jonathan. "We certainly will have a challenge to be fair about our observations. I know the Lord's hand is in His creation. Now, how can we observe and show this to the world?"

"Yes," responded Ann, "I feel the same way. I know one thing! I plan to study harder for these briefings than I ever did for anything in my life!"

"You can say that again," answered Jonathan. "I wonder if the Lord will allow us to see His handiwork in this new and exciting way?"

"Well, we know that He'll hear us if we pray about it," Ann reminded him.

Both Ann and Jonathan took time at the breakfast table to ask the Lord to give them guidance. They wanted to be sure that they would have His direction throughout the voyage. When they finished praying, Jonathan looked at his watch. "We'd better get going; its almost 0700 hours."

Drawing shows relative rotation and revolution of the earth and moon system. What does this mean to an observer on earth? The answer is on the next page.

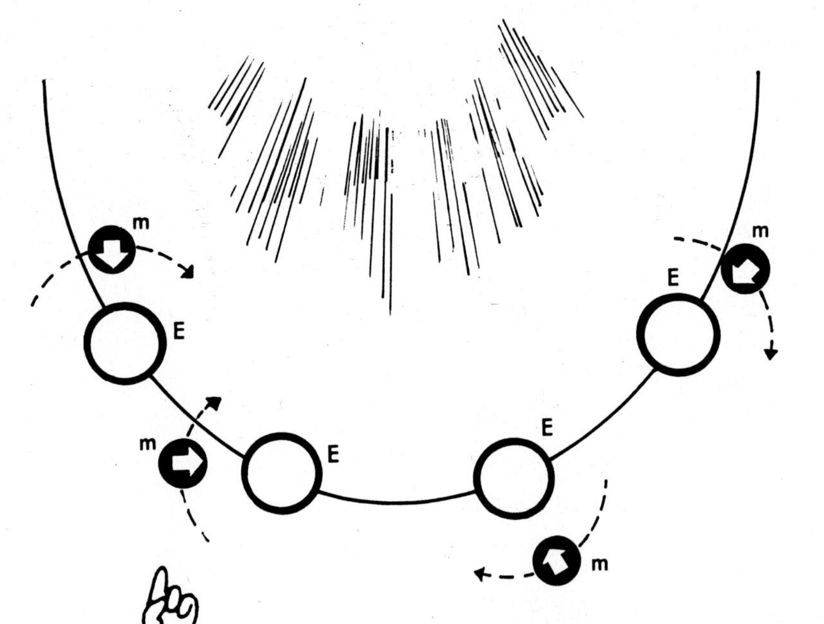

They hurriedly finished their breakfast, put their trays away, and started for the planetarium building.

They met Captain Venture standing at the door. "Good morning," he greeted them. "Are you ready for the next session?"

"I guess this session will be about the planet Mercury, won't it?" asked Jonathan.

"You're right, Jonathan," the captain answered. "We'll start with that tiny, hot-and-cold planet in the briefing today."

Ann and Jonathan took their seats in the briefing room as Ann commented, "I've always wondered how we could view the planet Mercury for any length of time. It seems to me that the astronomer's telescope would always have to be looking into the sun."

"Well, Ann," answered the captain, "you're right in one way. We can only see the planet Mercury early in the morning and again in the evening, but now astronomers have filters which they can place on their telescopes so they can look directly at the sun through its glare during the day. I have to add that, even then, Mercury isn't easy to see."

"I guess that's the reason we don't really know too much about this planet, right Captain?"

"That's right, Jonathan. There are some other things about the planet that hinder our viewing, also. For example, it takes Mercury 59 days to rotate on its axis and 88 days to revolve around the sun. It is similar, but not exactly, to the revolution and rotation of our own moon. You can imagine that this doesn't give us a lot of time for actual viewing of all sides of Mercury."

"I guess it's almost like our moon. The moon takes the same amount of time to rotate on its axis as it takes to revolve around the earth so we only see one side," Jonathan went on to comment.

"Yes," responded Ann, "but in spite of our difficulties in seeing it, we know that it takes Mercury 59 days to rotate on its axis and 88 days to revolve around the sun."

"Well, that's almost correct, except that we can see all sides of Mercury at one time or another," the captain explained. "But the relatively small difference between the periods means it takes a lot of viewing over a long time to be able to examine the whole planet."

"I read in the library yesterday that the temperature on Mercury is about 430 degrees Centigrade (Celsius)," commented Ann.

"Yes, but that's only part of it, Ann," volunteered Jonathan. "I read that on the portion of the planet facing away from the sun the temperature is about minus 170 degrees Celsius."

"Why should there be such temperature extremes, Captain?" asked Ann.

The captain smiled. "Jonathan, do you know the answer to that?"

"I think I know why this could be true," answered Jonathan. "I read that Mercury doesn't have an atmosphere, and if that's true, the heat on the sun side of Mercury wouldn't have anything to hold it in."

"Oh, that's right. I remember reading that too," said Ann. "That's why our atmosphere is so important to us. It holds the heat in. Isn't that right, Captain?"

"That's right. You'll also find out when we get to Mercury that the lack of atmosphere will make it a risky place for us to stay around for very long."

Ann asked the captain what the temperature would be like on Mercury if the planet rotated and revolved in the same period of time.

The captain's response was in the form of a question. "What do *you* think it would be like, Ann?"

"Well," she frowned in concentration, "if Jonathan's idea about the atmosphere is right, then that would only make the hot side hotter. I figure that if the same side always faced the sun, and Mercury is less than one **AU** from the sun, then its hot-side temperature would be much hotter than 400 degrees Centigrade."

"And the cold side would even be a little colder," Jonathan added.

"That's right," replied the captain.

The captain was called out of the room to answer a phone call for a moment, and the young people sat quietly thinking about their upcoming voyage.

When the captain returned, Ann voiced some questions that had come to mind:

"Captain, what will happen to us when we bring our shuttle craft into the area so near our sun? Will we be able to stand the extreme temperatures? The temperature on Mercury will be around 400 degrees Centigrade—much hotter than boiling water!"

"Yes, you're right about the temperature. We're going to have to protect ourselves inside the spacecraft. We'll be using special reflecting technology to keep the spacecraft from burning up, and we also have a backup cooling and heating system inside the shuttle for our additional protection," said the captain.

"Boy, I guess we won't be doing any space walking when we visit planet Mercury, Jonathan," quipped Ann.

"That's right, Ann," commented the captain. "We'll be operating our special equipment by remote control from the safety of the flight deck."

Jonathan wondered if the **spectrograph** could pick up special elements and gases if they were on

A spectrograph analyzes the light waves given off by different elements. These spectra show that every element has a different "fingerprint."

the planet. Captain Venture seemed to be thinking the same thing. "We'll be carrying a **spectroanalyzer** with us. This will enable us to see if there are small amounts of gases on the planet."

"We also should be able to detect surface metals with it, shouldn't we?" asked Ann.

"Yes. We can do this when we get close," answered the captain. "One other thing you'll be interested in," added the captain, "is

The magnetometer is a very special instrument that enables scientists to detect the strength of magnetic fields very precisely.

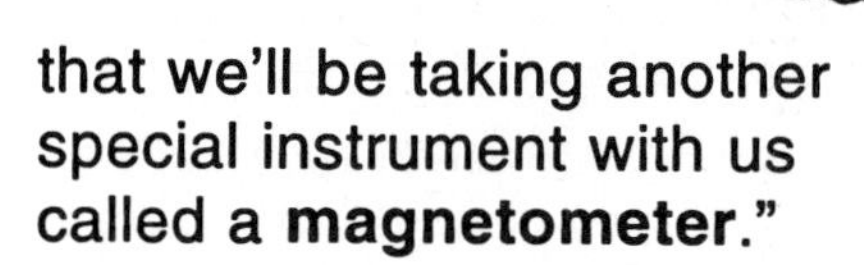

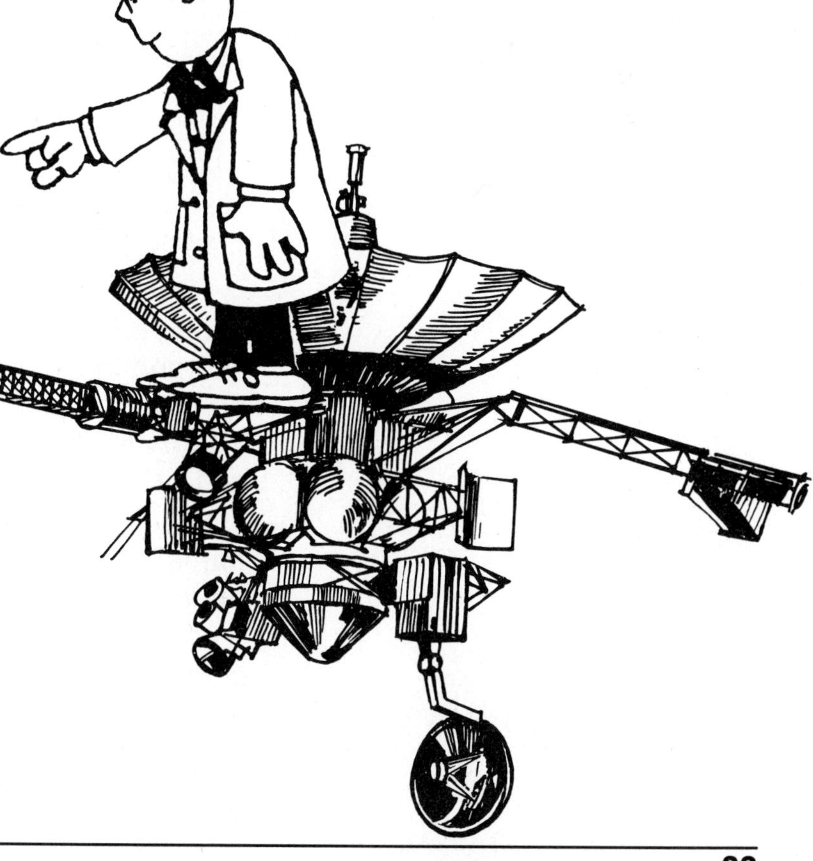

that we'll be taking another special instrument with us called a **magnetometer**."

"A **magnetometer**!" exclaimed Jonathan. "What's that?"

"I know it has to have something to do with magnets, doesn't it?" asked Ann.

"In a way that's correct, Ann, but the magnet it deals

with is the planet's magnet."

"I never knew a planet *had* a magnet," commented Jonathan.

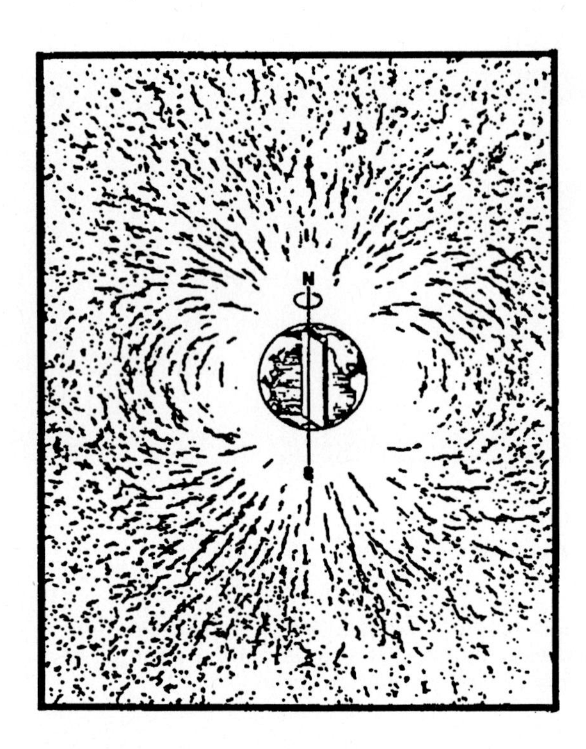

The earth has a huge magnetic field. The planets will be tested for their magnetic fields during the voyage. This picture shows iron filings around a bar magnet to illustrate this.

"Well," added the captain, "some do. In fact, our earth has a very large magnet that has been getting weaker over the years.

"But we'll be talking about this when we get to our study of the earth. The **magnetometer** is an instrument that helps us measure a magnetic field. We can find out some interesting things about a planet just by measuring its magnetic strength, and we'll be learning more about this when we get close to the planet. At the moment, Mercury doesn't appear to be a very exciting planet, but who knows what we'll find when we get there. There have even been some indications of ice caps at the poles. We are going to have to examine these carefully when we get there. There is some rumor that the caps at either pole might be made of different materials."

"The pictures I've seen of Mercury remind me of the moon with its craters," commented Ann.

"I'm anxious to find out what's there when we get a close-up view," added Jonathan.

Captain Venture asked the two young astronauts if they had any more questions about Mercury. They seemed satisfied with what they had learned and had no more questions, so the captain told them to take a 15-minute break and to be back in the briefing room at 1345 hours.

"Our next topic will be on the planet Venus, named after the Roman goddess of love and beauty," he informed them as they were going out the door.

The young people wasted no time getting to the cold-drink machine down the hall, and they had much to say about the upcoming briefing on Venus.

"I always thought of Venus as the sister planet of the earth," said Ann.

"The first thing that comes to my mind about Venus is the Roman goddess of gardens and spring," countered Jonathan.

"Isn't Venus the planet that's called the 'morning and evening star'?" asked Ann.

"That's what I've heard," answered Jonathan. "I remember watching Venus through our astronomy club's ten-inch telescope. It seemed bigger to me when it was in the crescent stage than when it was in the full stage."

"I think the reason for that," commented Ann, "is that when Venus is in the crescent stage, it's closer to us in its orbit around the sun."

"Yes, I guess so," said Jonathan. "I never thought of that."

"By the way," added Ann, "did you know that Venus rotates backward?"

"Yes," answered Jonathan, "that's called retrograde motion."

Ann checked her watch. "We'd better get back to class or the captain will be upset," said Ann, hurrying down the hall. They dropped their cans in the recycling container and headed for their seats in the briefing room.

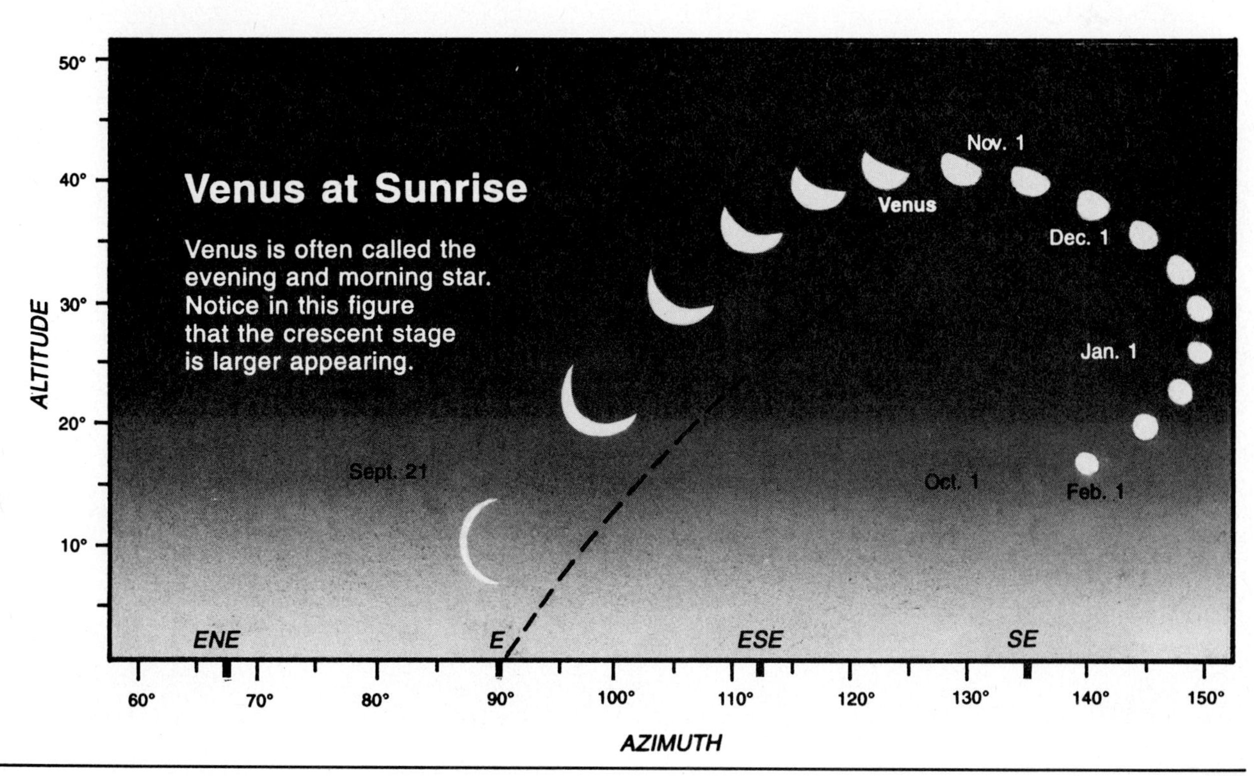

Questions

1. Make a case for creation based upon what you have already learned about Mercury.
2. Make a prediction about the possibility of life on planet Mercury.
3. In your own words, give your first impression of Mercury.
4. Explain what is meant by a planet's magnetic field.

This three-dimensional representation of the Magellan radar image of the Golubkina Crater image on planet Venus. This crater is 34 kilometers (20.4 miles) in diameter. No doubt the crater was caused by a large meteorite impacting the planet. (NASA photo)

"Well, Kids, I have to compliment you on your punctuality," the captain greeted them as they took their seats. "We have some interesting things to talk about concerning this next planet. Venus, as well as most of the other planets, is much brighter than any of the stars. When we talk about a planet's **apparent magnitude**, you'll find it's almost always a minus number.

MAGNITUDE SCALE

Apparent Magnitude Difference In Star Brightness

Magnitude Difference	Brightness Factor
...	...
0	1.00
1	2.512
2	6.31
3	15.85
4	39.81
5	100.00
6	251.20
7	631.00
8	1585.00
9	3981.00
10	10,000.00
11	25,125.106
...	...

Most of the planets are so bright they wouldn't even fit on this star-brightness scale. Imagine Venus with a -4.4 and Mercury with a -1.9. You will notice that this scale is similar to the scale on a thermometer. We have only defined the space between the marks on the scale.

"In the case of Venus, it's minus 4.4, as compared to Mercury's minus 1.9. You can see that Venus is much brighter. There are other characteristics about this planet you also need to know. Can either of you tell me about these?"

"I've read that the atmospheric pressure on the surface of Venus is many times that of the earth," commented Jonathan. "Is that right, Captain?"

"That's right, Jonathan. The scientific readings that we're getting seem to indicate that its atmospheric pressure is 90 times our pressure here on Earth."

Ann gasped! "Ninety times! The earth's atmospheric pressure is 14.7 pounds per square inch at sea level. Imagine what the pressure on Venus is!"

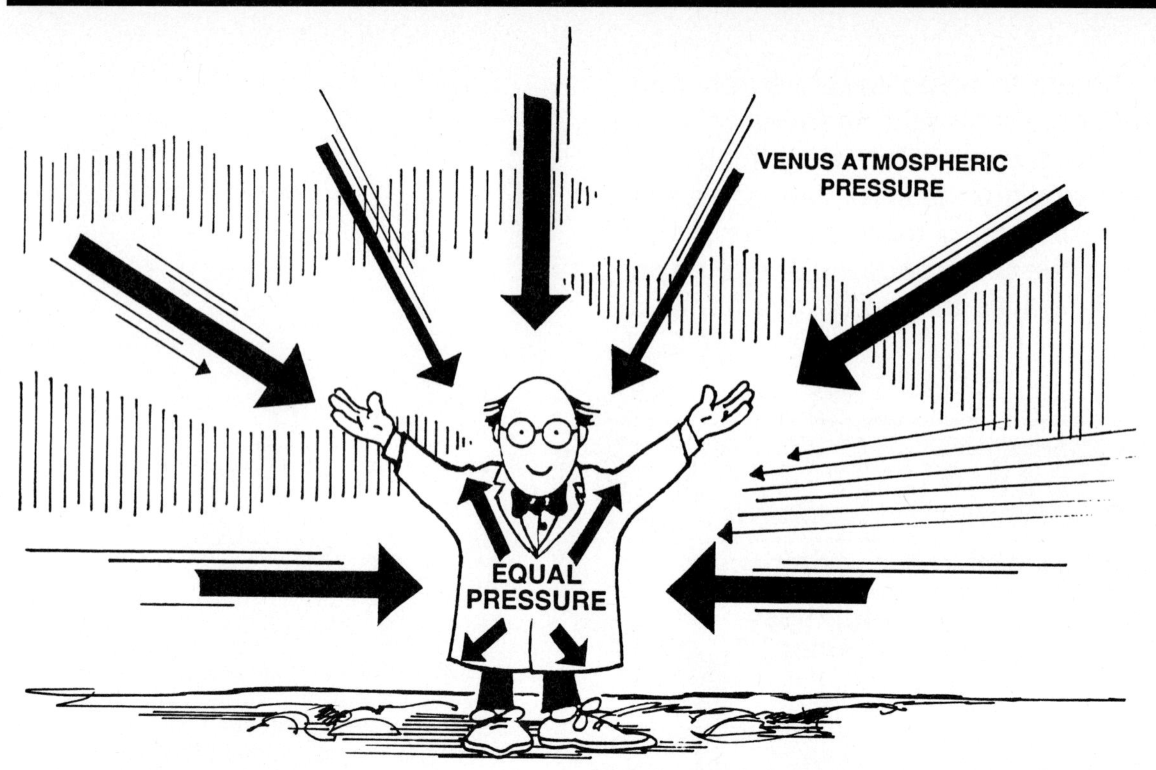

The atmospheric pressure on Venus would be so great our bodies would have to compensate for the increased pressure.

"Well, 14.7 x 90 equals 1,323 pounds per square inch," stated Jonathan. Of course these are "ballpark" figures.

"I hope we aren't planning to land on Venus, Captain," shuddered Ann. "We'd get crushed if we did."

"No, we aren't, Ann, but not for that reason alone. Venus is a planet with other severe conditions. It has a temperature of about 480 degrees Centigrade (900°F), which is hot enough to melt lead," said the captain.

"Venus is the hottest planet in the solar system, and we can see that it's much hotter than the planet Mercury, even though it's twice as far away from the sun. I'd like to challenge both of you with this question: Why do you think this is so?"

"I have an idea, Captain," commented Jonathan. "We know that Venus has a thick atmosphere. Is it possible that the sun's rays hitting the planet's atmosphere cause a runaway **greenhouse effect**?"

Turning to Jonathan, Ann asked, "What do you mean by **'greenhouse effect'**? I've heard about this, but I've never had it explained to me."

The captain stepped up to the chalkboard. "Let me explain this to both of you. The **greenhouse effect** is something we've been hearing much about. It works something like this:

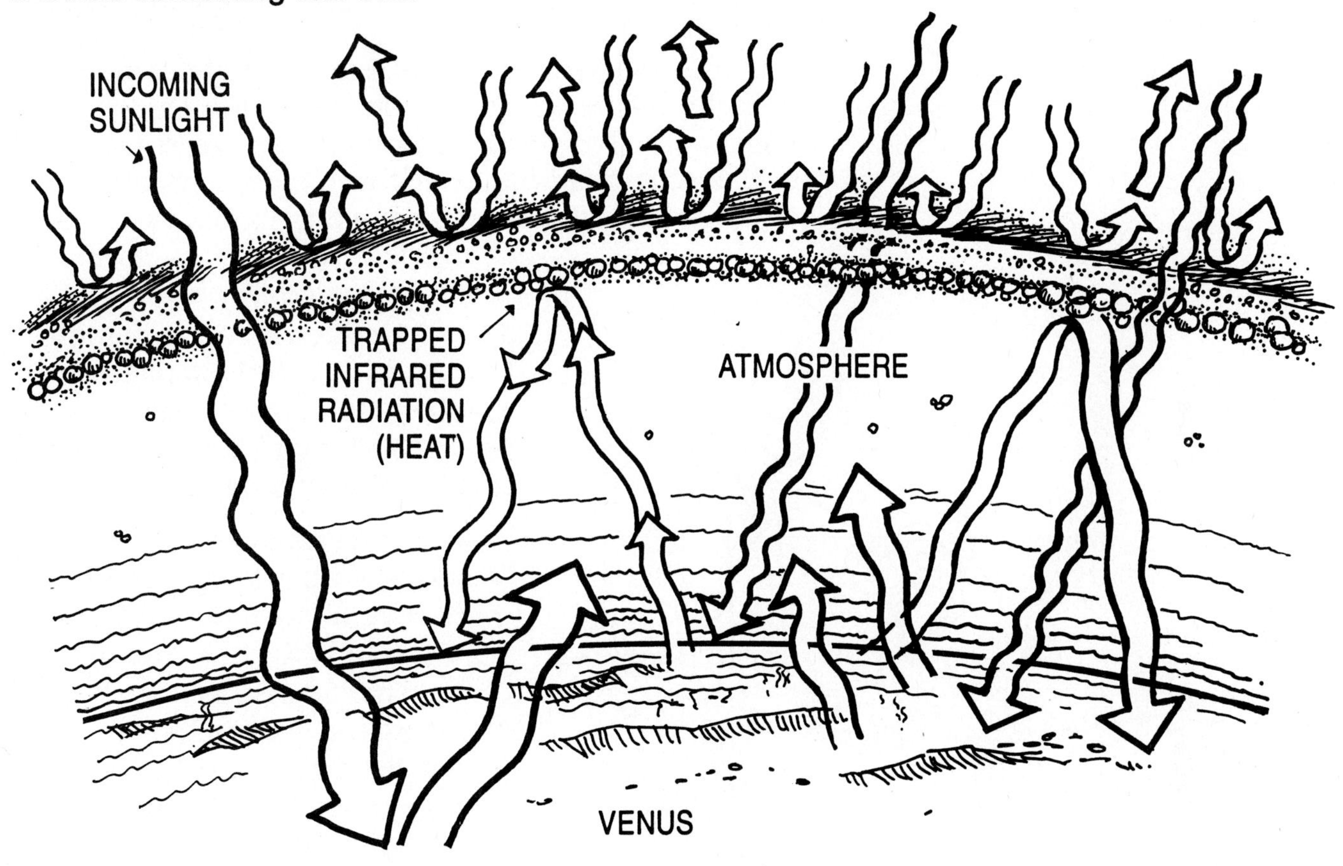

The "greenhouse effect." Notice the long penetration rays do not escape from the planet after they penetrate the atmosphere. They are trapped inside.

"When the rays of the sun penetrate the atmosphere of a planet, some of the rays—the long, infrared rays of the spectrum—can't bounce back out and are retained within the planet's atmosphere, thereby increasing the heat on the planet's surface."

The captain demonstrated the idea by sketching it on the board.

"I've heard that carbon-dioxide gas also has a lot to do with the **greenhouse effect**, Captain, is that true?" Jonathan asked.

"Yes, it does, and this is something else interesting about the Venus atmosphere; it's loaded with carbon dioxide. In fact, our instruments here on Earth tell us that its atmosphere is about 95 percent carbon dioxide. This gas is the perfect gas to cause the **greenhouse effect**. That compares with our atmosphere on Earth, which is only about 0.03% carbon dioxide.

In fact, we here on planet Earth are concerned about the buildup of carbon dioxide in the earth's atmosphere. Too much carbon dioxide could cause our planet to overheat, which would do considerable harm. Ice caps at the poles could melt, oceans could overflow, and a host of other calamities could occur."

"Just because the carbon dioxide in the atmosphere increased?" asked Ann.

"Well, that's a good part of it," replied the captain.

Jonathan asked if there was any truth to the rumor that the atmosphere of Venus had acid in it.

"That's not a rumor, Jonathan," replied the captain. "Our instruments here on Earth show that there are a number of acids in the Venus atmosphere. In fact, some of the strongest acids that we know of, such as sulfuric acid and hydrochloric acid, are present. In fact, another strong acid, hydrofluoric acid—so strong it can etch glass—is also present. But we'll find out more about that when we orbit the planet in the space shuttle. We know there'll be some surprises for us when we arrive, so just be expecting them.

Acids are corrosive.

"Well, kids, that ends our briefing on the inner planets. Before I dismiss this briefing, though, I want to give you a little idea of what our topic will be about tomorrow. We'll be studying Mars—the nearest outer planet to the earth."

"Won't we be getting briefed on planet Earth, Captain?"

"We certainly will, Jonathan, but that will be the last planet in our briefing."

"I know why that is," volunteered Ann. "That's so we can compare our planet with the others at the very end."

Captain Venture smiled. "That's one of the reasons, Ann, but there's another. Can you think of what it might be?"

"Is it because the earth is a very special creation?" asked Jonathan.

"That's precisely it, Jonathan," said the captain. "Everything we know about the earth is that it's unique in comparison to the other planets. We should see this when the earth briefing session comes up.

"I think we'll stop for today, but I want both of you to go to the library and get ready for our briefing on Mars tomorrow."

Ann and Jonathan walked out of the room in a quiet mood.

"Doesn't the subject of Mars give you a strange feeling?" asked Ann.

"In a way it does," commented Jonathan. "I always think of Mars and little green men."

Ann laughed. "I know what you mean. I've read about the Viking spacecraft that landed on Mars in 1976. Back then scientists were anxious to see if Viking was going to reveal anything about Mars that would help support the theory of evolution. It's wonderful that God has given man the means to search out the universe and explore this creation, but it's amusing to see how man uses this ability in the hope that he'll be able to prove the Bible wrong. Many of the scientists were really disappointed that Viking couldn't find life on Mars."

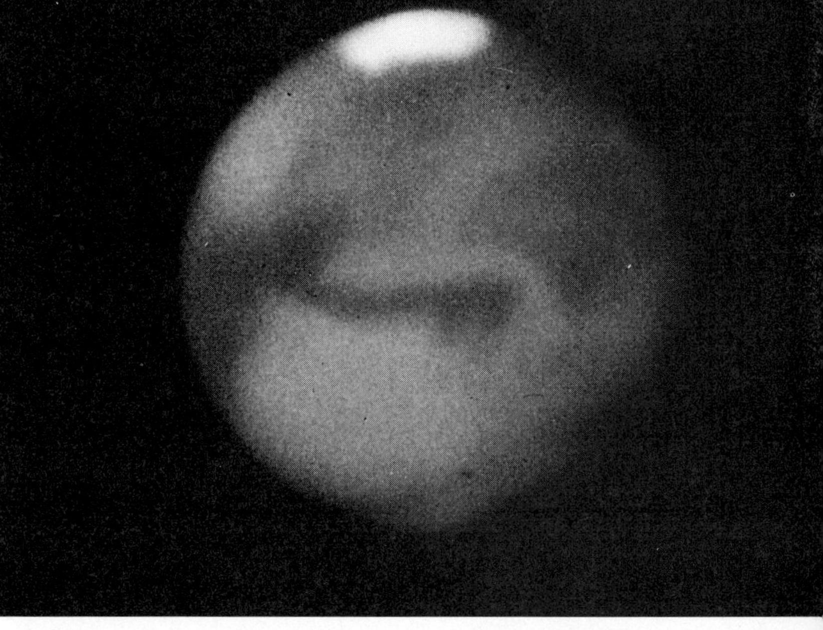

Mars (NASA)

"What if we did find life on Mars, Ann? Would that prove the Bible to be wrong?" asked Jonathan.

"Of course not!" exclaimed Ann. "Men have always tried to use new scientific discoveries to discredit the Bible, but the Bible has always proven itself in history. Often scientists jump too fast on meager evidence and then become embarrassed in the end. And God's creation is clearly stated in the book of Genesis, and we can count on that. So far, it appears that the Creator did not create life elsewhere, and it certainly did not evolve on other planets."

"Yes, I guess you're right on that score," pondered Jonathan. "It's easy to say, 'What if?' about almost anything. Sometimes we let our 'what if's' get in the way of true science, don't we?"

"I'll say we do," sighed Ann, "and these theories are loaded with assumptions."

Questions

1. From what you have found out about Venus so far, make a case for creation.
2. What can you say about the atmospheric pressure of Venus?
3. What can you say about the temperature of Venus?
4. Explain the "greenhouse effect" in your own words. Which gas contributes most to the effect?

CHAPTER 4

OUR CREATOR'S PLANET MARS

Later, the young people were doing their homework research on Mars in the academy library when Ann whispered, "Hey, Jonathan, did you read about Percival Lowell, the amateur astronomer?"

"Yes," answered Jonathan. "This guy really got excited about life on Mars."

"It says here," added Ann, "that he was one of the astronomers who misinterpreted the Italian name 'canali,' which means channels in English, to mean canals."

Jonathan laughed softly. "I think he was so anxious to see intelligence on the planet he couldn't resist the idea."

"From what I read about Lowell, he even wrote a book entitled *Mars*. All of the scientists were excited when Mars came into **opposition** back then."

"Explain the word '**opposition**' to me, Jonathan. I never really understood it."

"In the simplest terms, all it means is that a planet, in this case Mars, is passing through a point opposite the sun on the outer side of the earth. It gets more complex when you hear the astronomer talk about **favorable opposition**. What he means here, is that the planet is at **perihelion**, or closest to the sun, while at **opposition**."

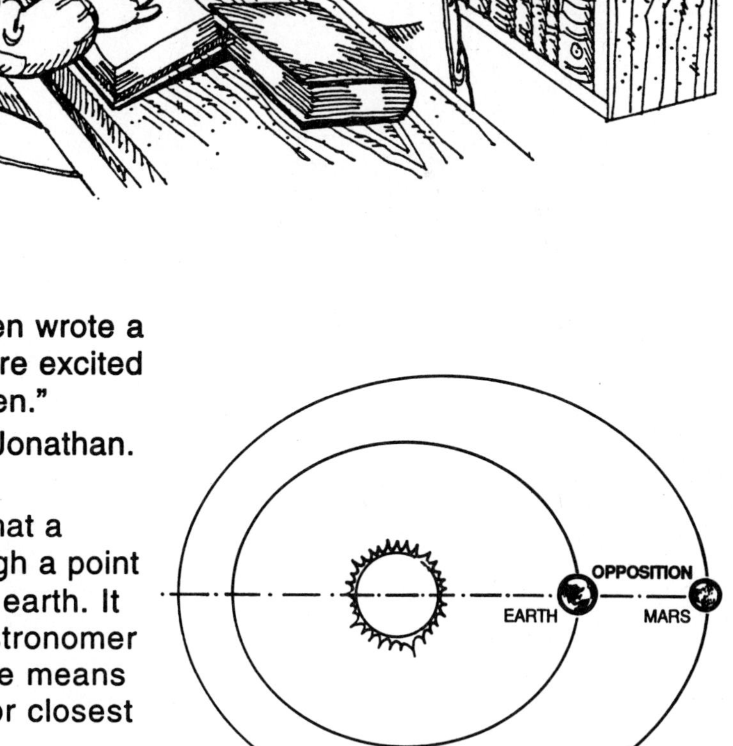

This shows the planet Mars at opposition.

Ann shook her head from side to side. "Oh, that's getting too complicated for me!"

"Well, I'm glad we have more scientific information about Mars than Lowell and others had back in

1896," Jonathan responded. "When you think about it, we didn't know much about this planet until Mariner and Viking spacecrafts orbited and landed on the planet. I guess, when you think about it, it wasn't so unusual to have ideas like Lowell had back then."

"That's right. The Mariner probes were in 1965, 1969 and 1971, The Viking probes didn't come until 1976, and Pathfinder in 1997," added Ann.

"Yes, I know," Jonathan agreed. "We sure have a lot to thank NASA for. Our space program gives a lot of benefits that we don't always think about."

At that moment the lights blinked off and on in the light fixtures above them. Ann looked at her watch. "Is it time for the library to close already? I can't believe it's that late," she commented as she started to gather up her materials.

"Yeah, I guess we'd better close up shop and get to our dorm rooms in a hurry," yawned Jonathan as he stood and stretched. "I'm looking forward to our briefing session on planet Mars tomorrow. It should be a good one. I've already got some questions I need to ask the captain."

"Come on. I'll walk you to your dorm, and then I'll get to my own."

Almost before they knew it another day had dawned and they found themselves back in the briefing room.

"Well, well, good morning, fellow astronauts!" exclaimed the captain in greeting.

Both Ann and Jonathan smiled feebly. In the first place, they wondered how the captain could be so cheery and wide-awake at this unearthly hour, and, secondly, they never really thought of themselves as astronauts. Captain Venture was one, of course, but them? Not really!

"What did you get out of your library study last evening?" the captain asked.

"Well, we have a new appreciation for NASA and all the research that has come out of that program," commented Ann.

"And we found many more questions than answers," Jonathan added.

"I thought the information on the seasonal snow caps at both of the Martian poles was interesting," commented Ann.

Jonathan couldn't resist correcting Ann. "You mean frozen-water ice in the north cap and carbon-dioxide ice on the southern cap, don't you?"

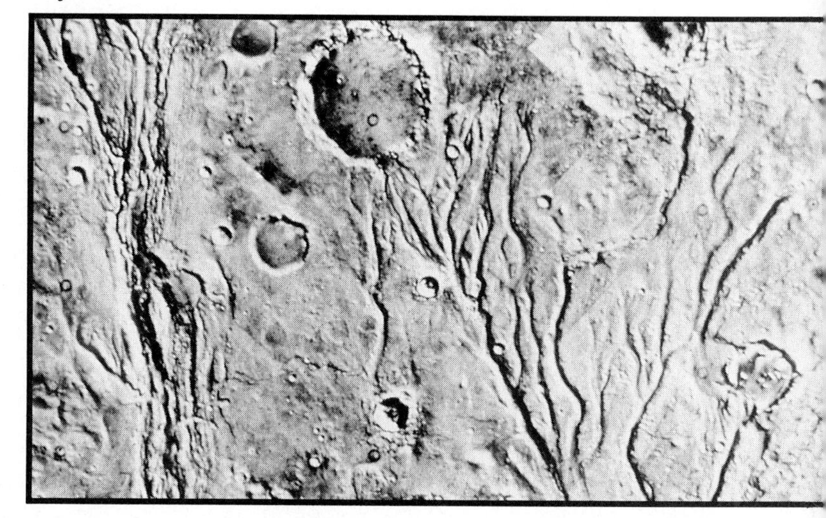

"Okay, okay, thanks for showing me up!" replied Ann. "I guess I am beginning to think like Percival Lowell and others back in 1896," she admitted sheepishly.

"Oh, this brings up an important point," the captain stated. "Thanks for reminding me. Scientists are just as guilty as the average person when it comes to making **assumptions**.

"They often get a little information and build a massive case around it, but, fortunately for science, there is always someone who questions those **assumptions**."

"The pictures we saw from the Mariner and Viking space probes showed many impact craters on the planet," commented Ann.

"There were several photos that showed signs of volcanoes, also," added Jonathan.

At this point, Captain Venture pulled down a detailed map of Mars, showing its main features. "As you can see, we have come a long way since Percival Lowell's day. We not only have a fairly detailed map of Mars, but Mars is one planet this expedition will get to know very well."

"I read about the Viking 1 lander taking samples of Mars' surface on July 20, 1976. The whole thing seemed so complicated and scientifically exciting. Could you explain this experiment to us?" asked Jonathan.

Captain Venture went to the chalkboard to show the details of this project. He pointed to the lander parachuting gently to the surface of the planet.

"From this point, we witnessed the most complex scientific operation I have ever seen in my career," explained the captain.

"Twin cameras went into operation to scan the surface of Mars for anything moving. After the cameras collected their information, a long scoop stretched out nine feet on the surface to scratch up a small amount of surface material. The arm was then retracted. With the soil in hand, it shook the material into the opening of the biology instrument."

The captain went on to explain the details of the experiment.

Jonathan and Ann were listening intently.

The captain showed why, at the conclusion of this elaborate experiment, scientists had to admit, scientifically, that there was no evidence of life on this red planet—planet Mars.

NASA

"I'm sure this will go on as long as man has a curious bone in his body," commented Ann. "It almost seems unimportant to talk about **Phobos** and **Deimos**."

"What's **Phobos** and **Deimos**?" asked Jonathan. Captain Venture explained that **Phobos** and **Deimos** are two tiny moons of Mars.

"**Phobos** is the larger," explained the captain; "it's only seventeen miles across, and **Deimos** is the smallest, being only nine miles across." He went on to point out that neither of the moons are round, and that a good telescope was needed to see them from the earth.

"Actually, they look like big potatoes," he said. "Mars is one planet we could go on studying forever."

At that moment Captain Venture was called away to attend an important meeting, so he dismissed the briefing fifteen minutes early.

Questions

1. Make a case for creation with Mars.
2. What person is associated with the word "canali"?
3. Do good scientists make dogmatic assumptions?
4. In your own words, describe the planet Mars.

CHAPTER **5**

OUR CREATOR'S PLANET JUPITER

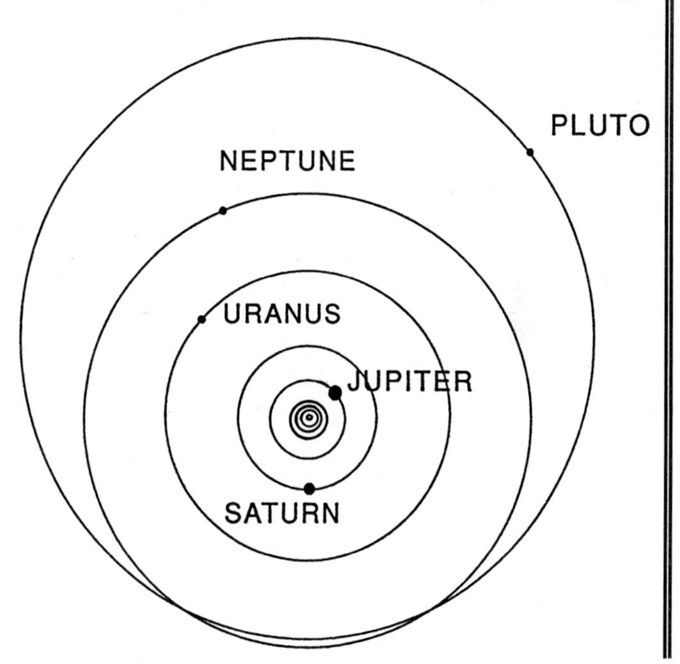

Ann and Jonathan met in the cafeteria for breakfast the next day, as usual. Ann seemed to have a lot on her mind. Jonathan's first comment when he sat down at the table was, "Well, are you ready for another big day?"

"Well, yes, and no," commented Ann vaguely. "I've been thinking about our topic for today and about all the other planets we've been studying. This whole thing is beginning to make me wonder about God's plan and purpose. He not only creates planet Earth for us to live on, but it seems that all the other planets we've been studying about somehow fit into His plan also."

"Ann," cautioned Jonathan, "remember what the captain said. Don't make any judgments until we've looked at all the evidence."

"I know, Jonathan, but here we are getting ready to study a planet that has a mass of almost 318 earths. In addition to this, it's composed of about 90 percent hydrogen and 10 percent helium, methane, ammonia, phosphene, water, and many other things."

"I know," answered Jonathan. "When you look at the chart, you can't help but wonder why it's even there. Any kind of life that *we* know couldn't even get started there."

"The only thing I can think of is that it's there to help us appreciate planet Earth more," concluded Ann.

"Well," added Jonathan, "I can see what direction this is taking us. It seems, as it does with everything else in the heavens, that God had a unique plan and purpose for every one—even this planet. I'm sure some of it will all become clear to us in time."

Briefing time came quickly, and the two young astronauts hurried to the room. Today they would be learning about the largest planet in the solar system.

Captain Venture entered the room with a big globe in his arms. He put it on the lab table in front of them and said, "This is planet Jupiter." He then picked up a tiny ball and said, "This is planet Earth. Can you imagine that our God of Creation thought more of this little planet Earth than He did of this giant one?"

Jonathan asked a tough question, which he knew the captain couldn't give a certain answer to. "Why did God do it this way, Captain?"

The captain thought awhile. "Have you ever considered that this might be one way for God to glorify Himself in the heavens?"

"I think I understand," said Jonathan. "God gave man a challenge to explore all of His creation. Look at the challenge it is giving us! The more we explore it, the more we recognize His greatness!"

"And this is only the tip of the iceberg," added Ann.

"Well, I can see that, once again, you've done your homework," commented the captain proudly. "This planet is an amazing planet to study. It has 16 moons that we know of, and it seems to be nothing but a ball of gas and liquid.

NASA

"Can you imagine a planet of this size with a surface temperature of about minus 250°F to over 45,000°F just outside the core?" asked the captain.

Jonathan thought about the captain's question. "It's hard to believe that anything can get that cold; it's even harder to believe that there is any possibility for life in such a place."

"There are some additional factors about Jupiter that I should mention to you," added the captain. "If there are seasons of any kind on Jupiter, the change is small. We can't even notice any variation from our telescopes here on Earth. This is one thing that we can check out further when we fly by the planet. However, you'll be interested to know that Jupiter has the shortest day in our solar system."

"An entire day and night on Jupiter is only nine hours and fifty minutes long. Just think how many more class periods we'd need to cover this material," commented Ann.

The captain laughed. "I think this is a good place to take our morning break, Kids. Let's dismiss for about 15 minutes. When we return, I want to take up the great red spot of Jupiter and the banding on the surface of the planet, and try to solve these puzzles."

As Jonathan and Ann drank their juice they discussed the topics they would be briefed on.

"I've often wondered about the red spot on Jupiter and always enjoyed watching it by telescope," said Ann between sips.

"So have I," stated Jonathan, "but we never stopped to think about what was causing it, did we?"

"I can say the same for the banding on Jupiter," commented Ann.

"I had an introduction to the light and dark belts," remembered Jonathan, "but never thought much about it, although I've read some recent research that indicates the light zones appear to be caused by rising air columns with clouds of ammonia."

"Jonathan," interrupted Ann looking at her watch, "it's time to get back to the briefing."

Color composite of the atmosphere of Jupiter (NASA).

They had no sooner sat down than the captain walked in. Jonathan was the first to speak:

"Captain Venture, Ann and I were discussing the red spot and the light-and-dark bands on Jupiter. Can you give us a clear explanation for either of them?" asked Jonathan.

"Well," answered the captain, "I don't know how clear my explanation will be, but the general view is that they are caused by strong **convection currents**. The lighter ones are hot and rising, and the darker ones are cooler."

"Well, that's what I was explaining to Ann, but I wasn't sure."

"The 'great red spot' is thought to have formed by one of the rising currents of warm atmosphere," continued the captain. He went on with his explanation by sketching on the chalkboard, showing how the 'great red spot' and the banding could be formed.

Ann had another question for the captain: "I've heard that all of the weather on Jupiter is formed in a 70-km-thick layer."

"I've seen those data, Ann. Seventy km is about 43.5 miles, so you can judge that this is a deep-weather system. There's much we don't know about this planet, so hold your theories about it lightly. Who knows what new information will come our way ten years from now."

"Speaking of new information, Captain," interrupted Jonathan, "I read that 22,000 km below the surface of Jupiter—that's over 13,000 miles—there are temperatures that reach 10,000 to 11,000 degrees Centigrade. Isn't this about the same temperature we find on the surface of the sun?"

"Yes, Jonathan, that's just about right, but you must remember that the sun is a star, and its overall temperatures are far greater than Jupiter's."

The captain went on to explain. It's likely that a central rocky core exists in Jupiter, but the evidence isn't certain.

Jonathan wanted to know about Jupiter's 16 moons. "Can you tell us more about them, Captain?"

The captain turned to the chalkboard again and started writing. While he was writing and diagramming on the board, he began talking about the diagrams:

"Jupiter has a satellite system containing four large moons about the size of the terrestrial or earth-like planets. It also has twelve confirmed smaller satellites.

"We wouldn't have this information if it weren't for Voyagers 1 and 2. These probes came very close to the planet, giving the Voyager an excellent opportunity to take great pictures.

"The four **Jovian moons** photographed by Voyager are really the only ones of any significance," said the captain. "They are named **Io, Europa, Ganymede**, and **Callisto**. They are known as the **Galilean Satellites**, since Galileo first saw them. Actually, there are four smaller moons that orbit even closer to Jupiter than these, and it gets even more interesting. Eight moons orbit much further out in two groups of four moons each."

"Whew!" exclaimed Ann. "I can't believe how complicated this is getting."

"Do you mean to tell us that Galileo, a creation-minded scientist, saw these satellites way back in the 1600's, Captain?" questioned Ann.

"That's right, Ann. He not only saw them and recorded them, but he did it with a telescope lens that wasn't much better than a piece of rough glass. Some scientists jokingly say he used a coke bottle for a lens."

"That gives us just a little idea of what careful observers these men were," added Ann.

Shows the giant volcano on the Jupiter satellite Io. (NASA)

The captain went on: "I should point out that many astronomers feel **Io** is the most volcanically active object in the whole universe."

"Yes," added Jonathan. "I read about how fortunate we were to have Voyager 2 fly by while it was erupting. They say its volcanoes spew out molten sulfur and sulfur dioxide."

"That would make it a poisonous satellite and also a terrible-smelling one," pointed out Ann.

The captain nodded and went on to explain that **Europa** has layers of water and ice, and also seems to be smooth. He explained that it seems to have no craters, and he went on to indicate that **Ganymede** and **Callisto** seem to consist of mostly ices. "This is probably why their densities are so very low," explained the captain.

Ann and Jonathan wanted to know more about the twelve smaller satellites.

"We don't know much about them," the captain told the young people. "They are well beyond the **Galilean** satellites and are insignificant, as far as we know. One interesting thing about them is that the largest ones orbit Jupiter in two groups of four.

"We owe so much to NASA and Voyager 2 for going out and getting this information for us, for we found out things about Jupiter that we would never have known.

"Who would ever have thought that Jupiter had rings? Yet the Voyager probes not only found rings that were less than 30km wide, or almost 19-miles thick, they even found a tiny satellite orbiting just outside the ring. It's truly amazing that we've been able to gather so much information about the most massive and beautiful planet in the solar system."

The curved edge is Jupiter's bright surface blocked to show the planet's faint rings. (NASA)

Questions

1. Using Jupiter, give a case for creation in your own words.
2. How many known moons does Jupiter have?
3. How high would an object bounce if it hit the surface of Jupiter? Why?
4. Name one significant thing known about Jupiter's red spot.

Color variations indicate different composition. (NASA)

Chapter 6

OUR CREATOR'S PLANET SATURN

"Now it's time to talk about Saturn," the captain said the next morning at the beginning of the meeting.

"That's our favorite planet after Earth," both Ann and Jonathan said at once.

"Yes, it's a popular and beautiful planet, all right, especially with its rings," the captain agreed. "It's sometimes called a 'gas giant,' along with Jupiter, Uranus, and Neptune. These outer planets are all much larger than the earth and do not have solid surfaces. Instead, they consist of many colorful but poisonous gases, such as **hydrogen**, **helium**, **methane**, and **ammonia**."

"What are Saturn's rings made of?" asked Jonathan. "Could I take a space-walk on them, and maybe take along my skateboard? I'm joking, Captain . . . I think!"

PLANETARY GAS NAME	CHEMICAL FORMULA
Hydrogen	H_2
Helium	He
Methane	CH_4
Ammonia	NH_3

"Well, Jonathan," laughed the captain, "those rings do look like a round sidewalk from the far-away pictures, but the set of rings is actually 102,000 miles wide and 330,000 miles around! It would take a long time to skateboard around those rings!

"Actually, though, the rings consist of a loose collection of rocks, boulders, and dust covered with frozen gases, or 'ices.'

"It's these rings that we'll concentrate on during our flight. The last space probe to Saturn was the Voyager probe, back in 1980. It sent back pictures of many distinct rings—some of them even 'braided' together. Our goal will be to note any changes in the rings. We'll count the rings and compare our findings with the Voyager number, and we'll also look for color and density differences.

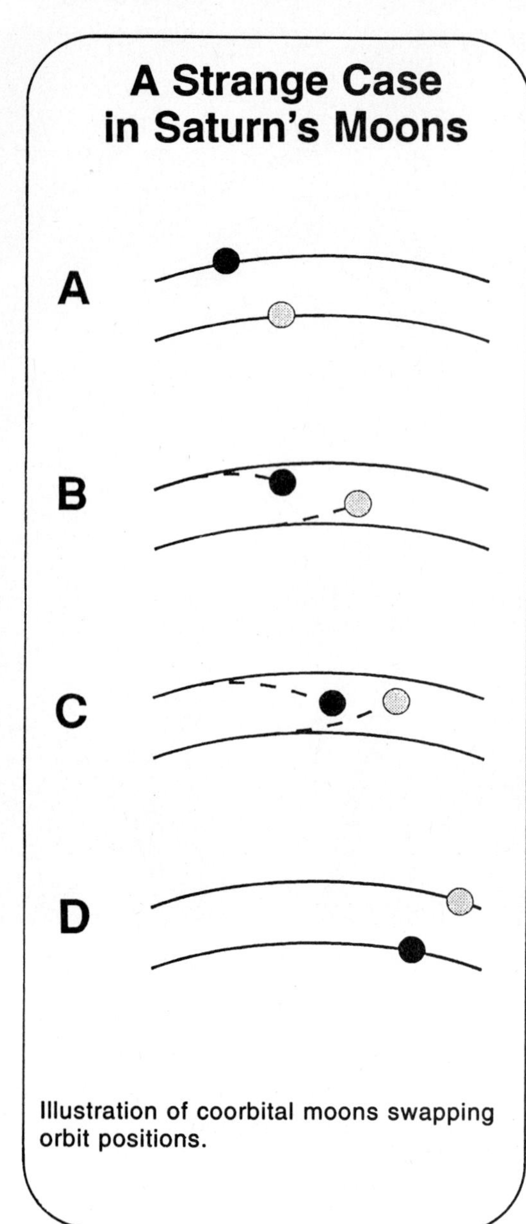

Illustration of coorbital moons swapping orbit positions.

"Finally, we'll look for evidence of the ring material slowly spreading out. There's a general tendency for objects in the universe to spread out and disintegrate. By the way Kids, you may have read that Saturn's **coorbital moons**, Janus and Epimetheus, actually trade orbits about every four years. The strange thing is that they don't collide or deflect each other out of their orbits. This seems to speak of plan and purpose, to my way of thinking. We're also learning that the solar system is an active, changing system. It seems that this also might indicate a recently created system, since an ancient solar system should have long ago settled down with an unchanging museum appearance. Well, I've popped a lot at you in a short time. I'm especially happy that you're both part of the space mission, because you're also young, and it seems we have a young solar system! It's time for some fresh ideas and recognition regarding God's creation."

"Thanks for the challenge," smiled Jonathan, and Ann agreed.

"We have a lot to learn, but you're a good teacher, Captain," stated Ann. "Giant Saturn will certainly stretch our thinking."

Jonathan's final comment before their being dismissed for the day was, "Can I take my skateboard along, just in case?" he grinned.

The captain knew Jonathan was teasing, so he just laughed as he left the room.

Questions

1. Could the coorbital moons of Saturn be evidence for creation? Give your reasons.
2. What is the creation significance of Saturn's rings spreading out?
3. How would the rings of Saturn affect theories?
4. What are Saturn's rings made of?

Chapter 7

OUR CREATOR'S PLANET URANUS

Ann and Jonathan came to class the next morning looking a little tired. They had stayed up quite late trying to get more information on the planet Uranus.

Uranus is a most exciting planet that has both orbital and rotational abnormalities which don't agree with any evolutionary explanation. (NASA)

Before the captain entered the room, Ann commented to Jonathan, "Doesn't it seem strange that until Uranus was discovered by Sir William Herschel in 1781, man knew only about the six planets out to Saturn? It took over two hundred years to find three more."

"Well," answered Jonathan, "I guess that's true, but even so, I can't help but think that ancient astronomers knew a lot about the sky. And Biblical history indicates that the astronomers of that day were well aware of the constellations and even the planets."

They both stopped talking when the captain walked into the room and threw out the first question.

"I want to hear the most impressive thing you learned about Uranus from your homework last night. Jonathan, you first."

"That won't be hard, Captain," answered Jonathan, "I was very surprised to learn that Uranus spins sideways. It seems like it's rolling at the same time its going around its orbit."

"They call this **retrograde motion**," Ann commented. "Uranus not only spins backward, but it is also tilted on its side. I think that's kind of strange, but something else struck me. Uranus takes over 84

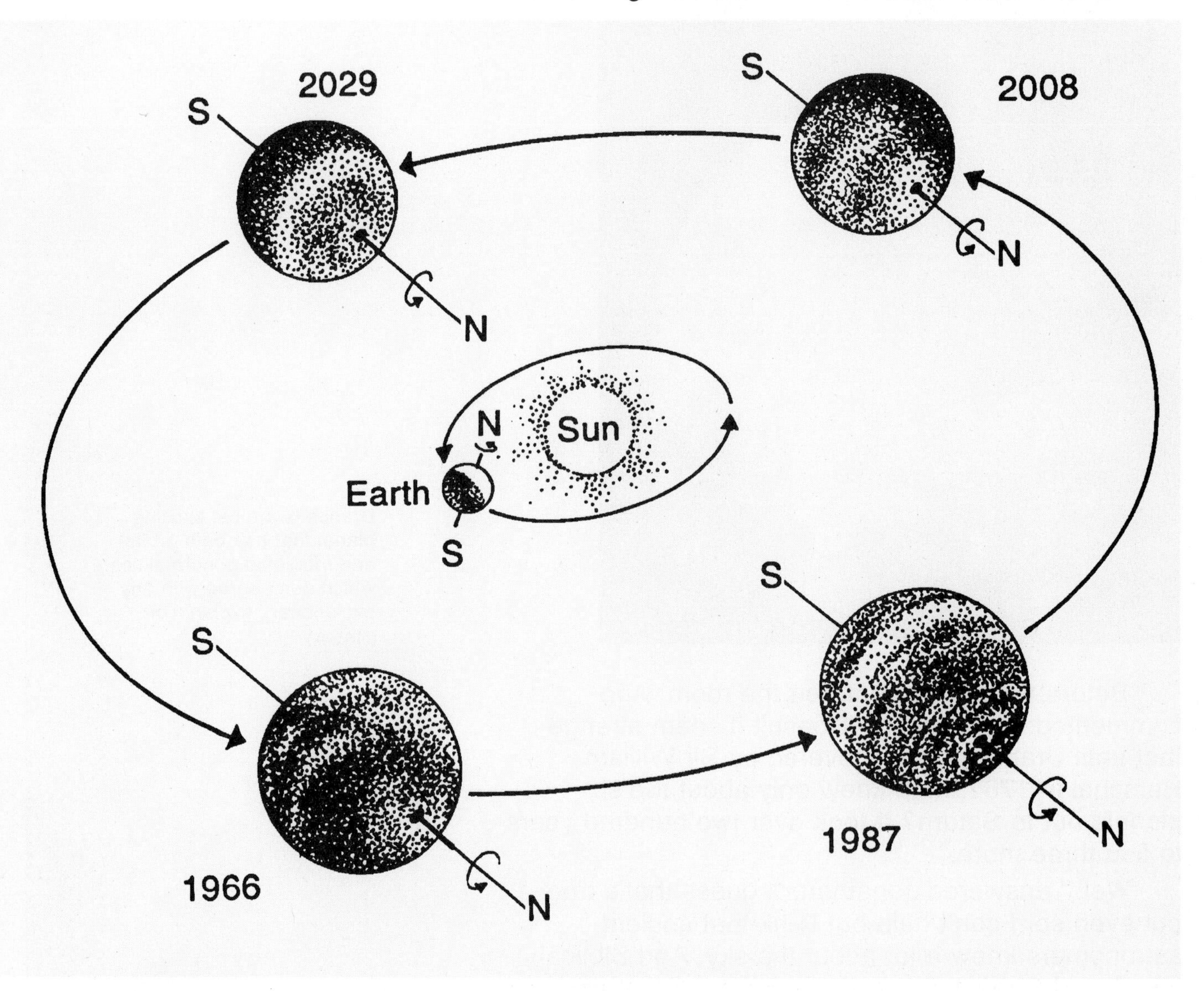

Uranus is spinning on its side and in reverse. This shows the 84 year orbit of Uranus compared to the earth.

years to orbit the sun. And another thing! There's a magnetic field on Uranus that is about 50 times as strong as ours here on Planet Earth."

"Why does the magnetic field interest you so much, Ann?" asked the captain, prodding her to deeper thinking.

Ann could see she was being tested by the captain on this point.

"Well, I remember your saying that a strong magnetic field could protect a planet from a lot of harmful radiation from the sun, so that caught my interest."

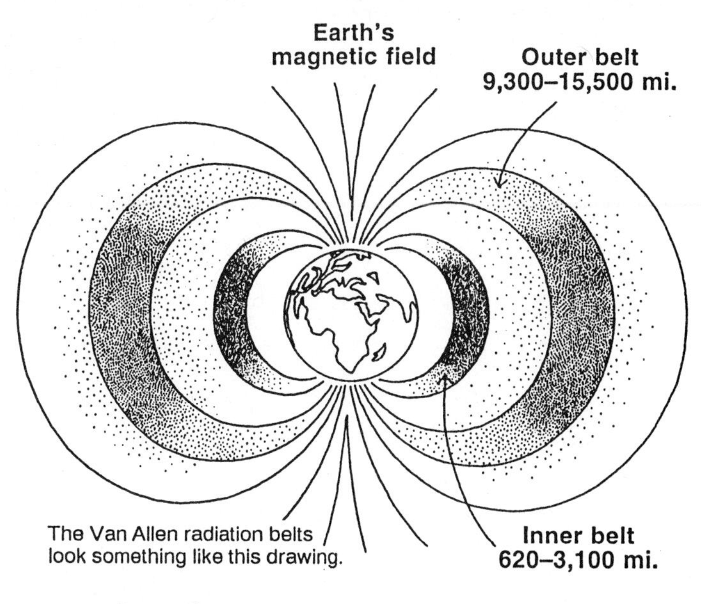

The Van Allen radiation belts look something like this drawing.

"You're correct on that point," said the captain. "Let me show you some things about the earth's magnetic field that might surprise you. Perhaps these same things might apply to planets such as Uranus. There are even more surprising things about the planet Uranus than we've been discussing here. Did you know that it has at least 15 icy moons?"

Jonathan did, and Ann didn't, and their heads nodded accordingly.

"Well, it does," laughed the captain.

"Another thing about this planet is that it has a thick atmosphere—one that you can't breathe. It's composed of methane and ammonia, and also has another gas called acetylene."

"Isn't that the gas that welders use in their torches?" asked Jonathan.

"That's correct, Jonathan," replied the captain.

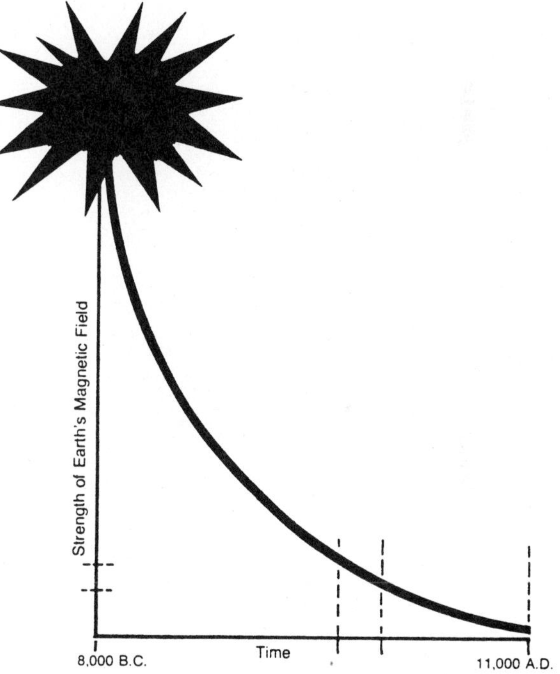

Suppose the earth's magnetism has been decreasing at a steady rate, then only a few thousand years ago the earth's magnetic field would have been too strong for any life. It would be as strong as some stars today (Dr. T. Barnes study).

Jonathan was anxious to make some additional statements about the planet. He had noticed that while the planet had a retrograde motion, its poles pointed toward the sun for many years at a time.

The Captain knew what Jonathan was thinking.

"Jonathan," the captain questioned, "do you think random processes of evolution such as a 'big bang' or something like that could have caused this?"

"No," responded Jonathan, "its just that this seems so strange to me. I don't know what to make of it. I know that this wouldn't happen normally."

Ann interrupted, "I think Jonathan is trying to say that this is a fingerprint left by our Creator."

"Yes," said Jonathan. "It seems that God is making His hand very clear."

"Well Kids," said the captain, "at least this is something we can think about. I'll see you tomorrow."

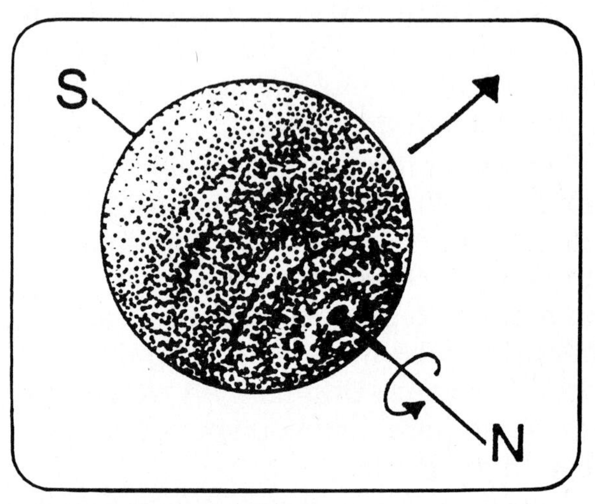

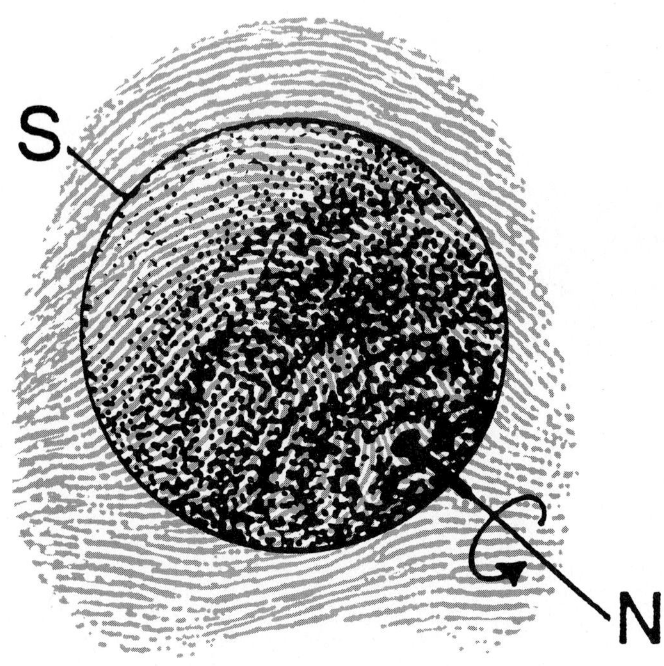

God's fingerprint is revealed throughout the universe in the unexpected, such as Uranus spinning on its side. He has introduced enough variety and surprise into the solar system that no natural-origin theory can provide an explanation.

Questions

1. See if you can make a good scientific case for creation using Uranus as evidence.
2. Explain how Uranus rotates on its axis.
3. How many moons does Uranus have?
4. What is the atmosphere of Uranus composed of?

Chapter 8

OUR CREATOR'S PLANET NEPTUNE

The young people walked over to the planetarium the next morning discussing all the information they had received so far. Ann was talking to Jonathan about the upcoming briefing session on Neptune.

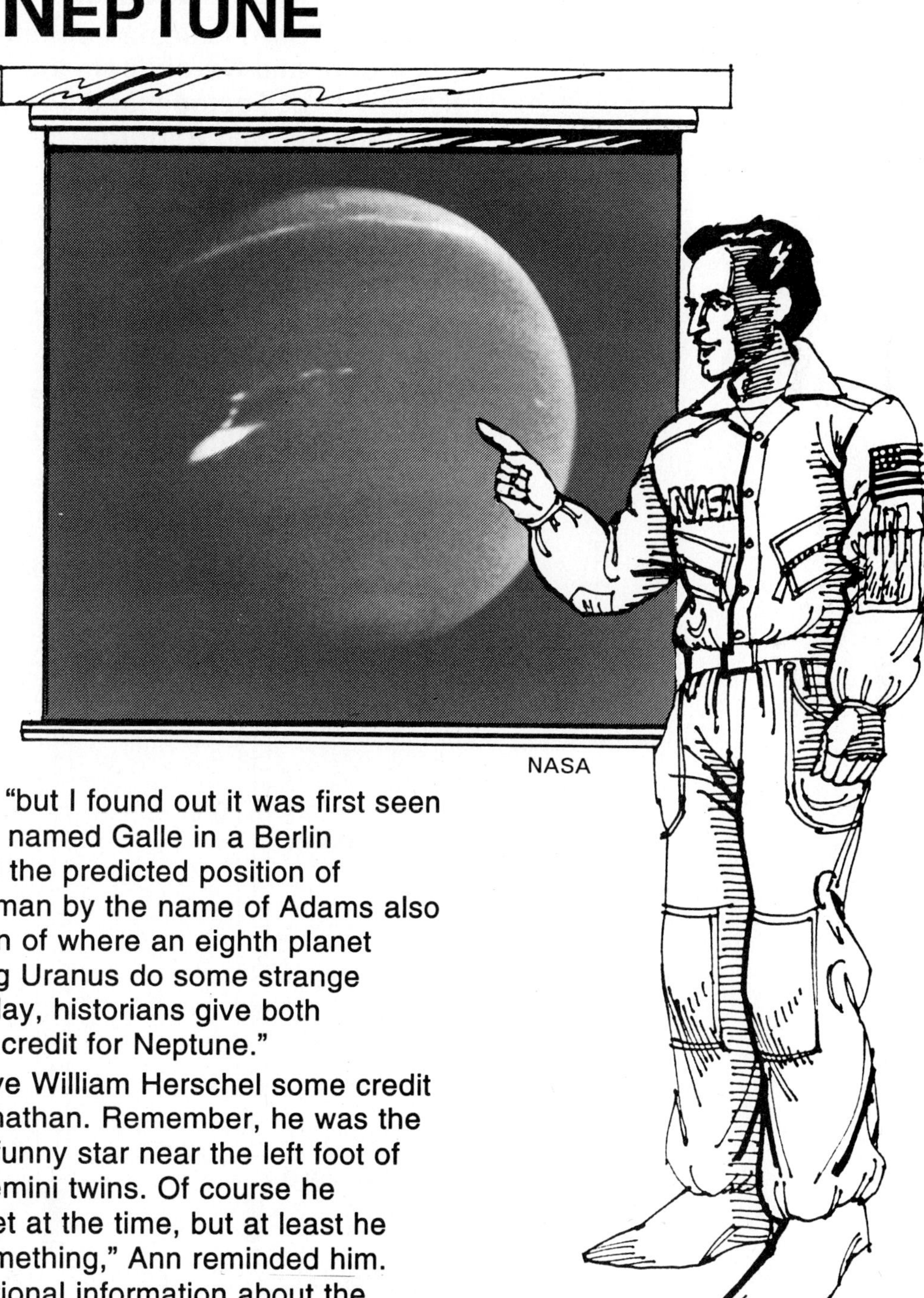

"I had a hard time finding much information on Neptune. Did you have any luck with your library research?"

"Not much," responded Jonathan, "but I found out it was first seen in 1846 by a scientist named Galle in a Berlin observatory. He used the predicted position of Leverrier. An Englishman by the name of Adams also calculated the position of where an eighth planet would be, by watching Uranus do some strange things in its orbit. Today, historians give both Leverrier and Adams credit for Neptune."

"Don't forget to give William Herschel some credit for this discovery, Jonathan. Remember, he was the one who noticed the funny star near the left foot of Castor, one of the Gemini twins. Of course he thought it was a comet at the time, but at least he called attention to something," Ann reminded him. "And I got some additional information about the planet. Neptune is always referred to as the eighth major planet. I also found that Neptune has eight moons—one of them, called **Triton**, the son of Poseidon in Greek mythology, is the larger. Another one is called **Nereid**."

"Do you suppose they were named after Greek goddesses, too?" asked Jonathan.

Ann's eyes widened, and she was quite impressed. "How did you know that?"

"Well, **Triton** is named after the sea god **Poseidon**, and **Nereid** from the Greek word for 'sea nymph.' I just figured that the Romans would have to get in the act with **Neptune**, the sea god in Roman mythology," laughed Jonathan.

"One other thing about **Neptune** that we'll need to know," added Ann, "is that its temperature runs at about 55^0K."

"Wow!" quipped Jonathan, "I guess we'd better take our coats with us."

The young people were already in their seats in the briefing room when the captain walked in.

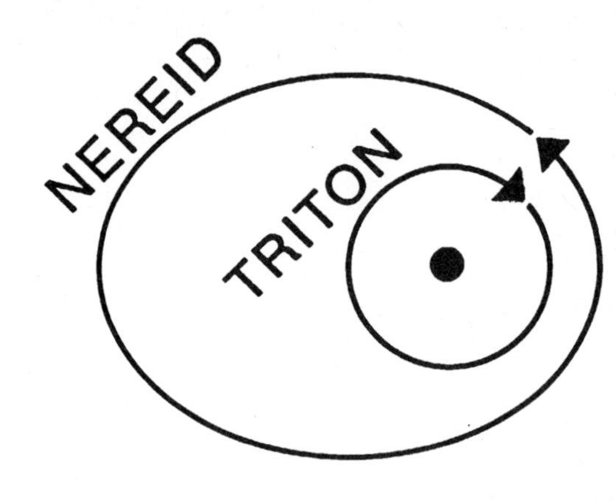

Showing the general relationship between the two principal moons (eight are present) of Neptune.

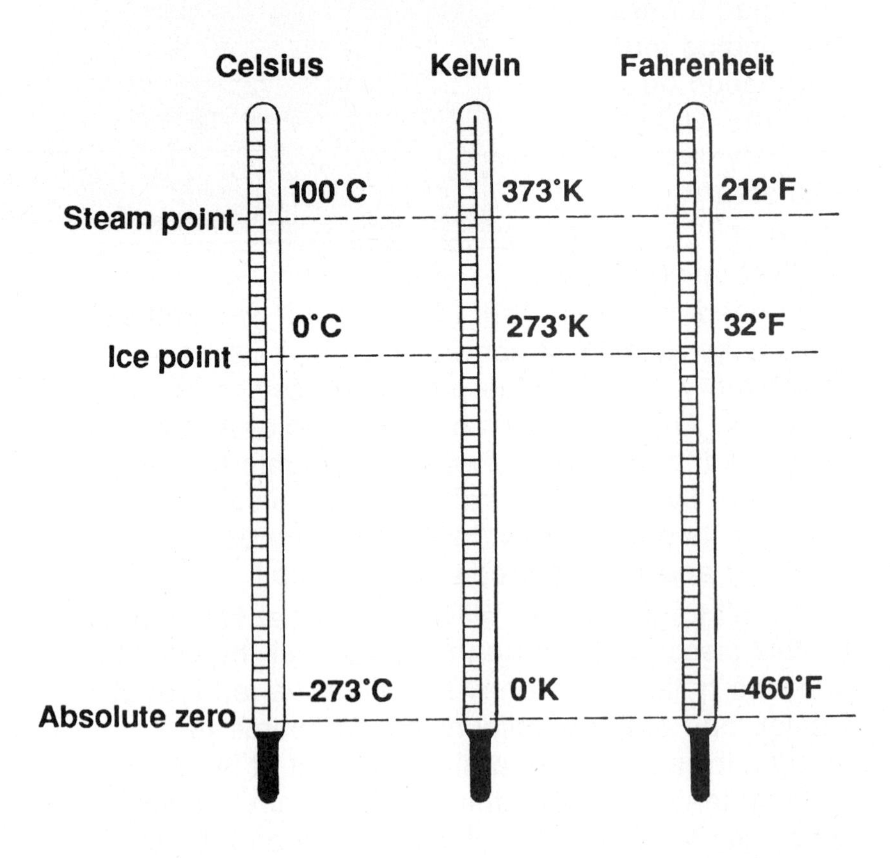

Comparison of the three most-used temperature scales in science.

"Well, how many rings does Neptune have?" he asked after greeting the young people.

Jonathan spoke up with a surprised look on his face. "Does Neptune really have rings, Captain? I thought there was still some question about that."

"Yes," spoke up Ann, "I thought so too." She looked at the captain with her head cocked to one side and grinned. "Is this a trick question, Captain?"

The captain laughed. "Well, maybe just a little," teased the captain. "But in one way you're both right. Voyager 2's passage through the Neptune area was to search for the possibility of rings. Some telescopes on the earth looked closely for stars that would blink as Neptune passed in front of them. One telescope

NASA

would see blinks and the other one wouldn't. Some scientists think the rings are in pieces, and that would account for some telescopes showing a star in the background blink while others didn't show it."

"It's just like unraveling a mystery," pondered Ann. "Scientists use all the most advanced technology to solve the mystery, and looking through a telescope for a blinking star seems to get the answer."

"Oh, just a minute now, Ann, it's not that easy," cautioned the captain. "All of the pieces to the puzzle come together a little at a time. That's what science is all about.

"One thing that does impress me is that all scientific investigation depends upon a universe that has much order. Scientists have to believe that the laws of science will be obeyed, and this certainly convinces me that an intelligent designer was behind all this. So, you see, I can't disagree with either of you on that point. The whole world of science would be non-existent if there were not some kind of order. These are good questions, Kids.

"But now I have an important meeting to attend, so we'll have to call it quits for today. See you at 0700 hours tomorrow."

Questions

1. Give your best creation argument for Neptune's existence.
2. How many moons does Neptune have?
3. In what year was Neptune discovered?
4. Describe the shape of Neptune's rings.

Chapter 9

OUR CREATOR'S PLANET PLUTO

After their greetings the next morning and some informal talk about how they had each spent their previous evening, the captain started right in.

"And now it's time for a preview of the last and smallest planet," said the captain.

"And that, of course, will be Pluto," piped up Ann. "Not only is it the last one we will be studying, because we've covered all the others, but we know that Pluto is the smallest planet and the farthest beyond the other planets—in fact, it's on the far edge of the solar system."

"Well, that's *almost* true," the captain continued, "but Pluto doesn't stay in one place. Its orbit takes it within Neptune's position, and then it does, indeed, move back out to the outermost reaches of the known solar system.

"Let me caution you, Ann, the solar system doesn't really have an 'edge.' The sun's gravity extends well beyond Pluto. Even greater, the entire universe is larger than the view of all our telescopes. There are probably vast areas beyond our imagination. Do you see what I mean?"

"Yes, I do, Captain. I'll be careful how I refer to 'edges' in the future," Ann responded.

"That's my flexible-thinking astronaut," the captain smiled. "But now, to get back to what we were saying:

"Until 1999, Pluto will actually be inside Neptune's orbit, although they are presently in different directions from the sun and are in no danger of colliding."

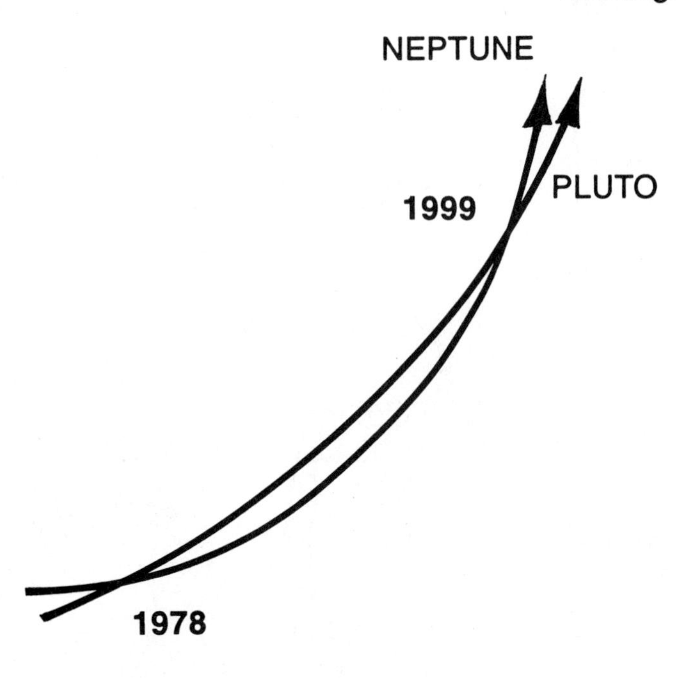

When Pluto is closest to the Sun, at perihelion, it is inside Neptune's orbit.

"With all the auto accidents we have here on Earth, I'm glad the Master Designer is driving those planets and not some woman or 'Mother Nature' down here," laughed Jonathan.

"Now just a minute!" Ann glared at him and playfully hit him lightly on the head with her notebook. "If I remember correctly, the last accident we saw just happened to be two *men* involved."

Jonathan laughed and ducked.

"Now, now, it's too early in the morning for me to be refereeing a fight," laughed the captain, "but I think Jonathan's point is a good one. It certainly would take a master planner and designer of infinite wisdom and intelligence and power to keep such a vast universe running smoothly and in order.

"Anyway," the captain grinned, "now that we've got the affairs of the universe straightened out, let's get back to what we were saying.

"The planet Pluto was discovered in 1930, but we've only been able to watch it move through one quarter of its orbit around the sun."

"Captain," asked Jonathan, "you're bringing up a point that I was wondering about. Our charts show that Pluto circles the sun once in 248 years, yet we've only known about Pluto for one-fourth of this time. Don't we have to wait for Pluto to completely circle the sun to measure its revolving time?"

"That's a good question," responded the captain. He then explained how Kepler's Laws of Motion make it possible to quickly determine an orbit's total revolving time. "Kepler was not only a scientist, he was a Christian, who lived four centuries ago, from 1571 to 1630. Through many years of study of planet data, he arrived at three fundamental laws of planetary motion. Although today we call them 'Kepler's Laws,' maybe they should actually be called the 'Creator's Laws.'"

KEPLER'S PLANETARY LAWS

FIRST LAW	Orbits are ellipses
SECOND LAW	Planets sweep out equal areas in equal times
THIRD LAW	$T^2 = CR^3$

T = Orbit Time
R = Average Planet-Sun Distance
C = A Constant

EXAMPLES OF KEPLER'S THIRD LAW

PLANET	ORBIT TIME IN YEARS	AVERAGE PLANET-SUN DISTANCE IN AU'S
MERCURY	0.24	0.39
VENUS	0.62	0.72
EARTH	1.0	1.0
MARS	1.88	1.52
SATURN	29.5	9.54
PLUTO	248.5	39.53

"Captain, I've been trying to find out what I could about this planet, and there's certainly not much we know about it," spoke up Ann, "but I did find out some things.

"First of all, it's probably covered with frozen, icy gases, since the temperature out there must be very cold, so how can our shuttle overcome such extreme temperatures?

"Second, a moon of Pluto, called **Charon**, was discovered in 1978.

"And, finally, Pluto seems out of place, since, even though it's small, it's located in the region of the large planets—the gas giants."

"There are many things about this planet we wish we knew," answered the captain. "Just think about its moon, **Charon**, for example. This moon is only six times smaller in mass than Pluto itself. Astronomers think this is too large for the size of the planet."

"And that's not all," added Jonathan. "Both **Charon** and Pluto are inclined more than 120 degrees in their orbits. . . ."

"And they both turn at the same rate, just like our moon does," interjected Ann.

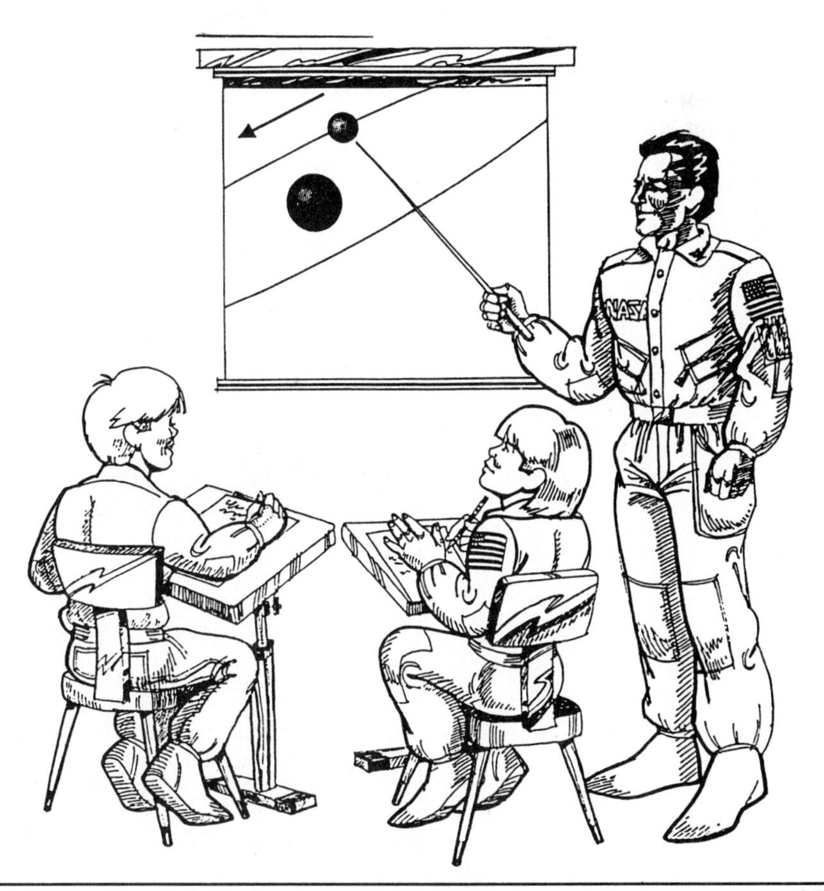

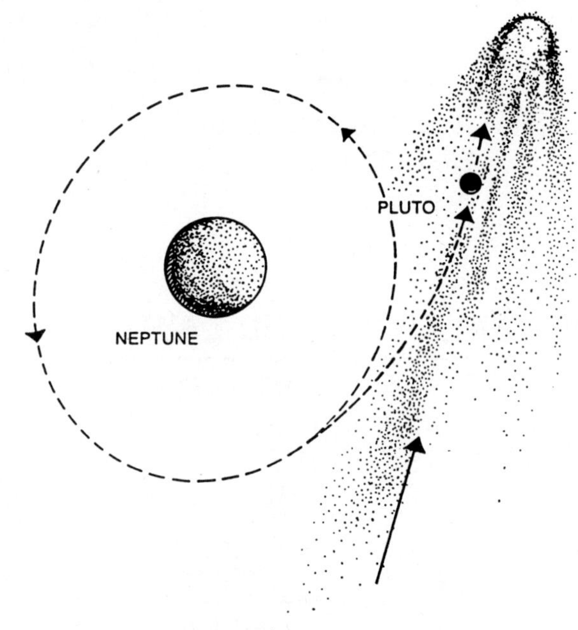

The theory is that a comet came close to Neptune's moon which was dragged away by gravitational attraction to become a new planet called "Pluto." This theory is generally held by astronomers in spite of the fact that there is no scientific evidence for the "Pluto" escape theory ever to have occurred.

"Well, I can certainly see you've both worked hard at your homework again," the captain smiled, "but there are many mysteries concerning Pluto. As you say, it's cold out by this planet—probably minus 380 degrees Fahrenheit, and it's also very dark out there. It definitely seems out of place, being the smallest planet in the outer realm of the 'major league' planets.

There has been some speculation that Pluto itself may be an escaped moon from another planet; so we'll be taking close-up pictures of the surface to further check this possibility. If this escape has indeed occurred, it shows that sudden, drastic changes, or catastrophes, may have shaped the solar system.

"We suspect that slow, gradual changes, such as evolutionists believe, are not true for the history of the planet Pluto," said the captain.

Ann was wide-eyed about the implications connected with little Pluto. "But Captain Venture, what good would it do to verify that Pluto was once a moon anyway?"

"Well, Ann, to verify that Pluto was once a moon also would shed light on one of the theories about the moon's origin. Some scientists have thought that the earth long ago *captured* our moon from somewhere else. However, if Pluto was once a moon, we then would have only evidence that moons *can escape* from planets—the exact opposite of *capture*."

The captain asked if there were any more questions, but all seemed satisfied that everything had been covered, so he dismissed the briefing, telling them that they would now be entering a new phase of their training, which was to start immediately.

Questions

1. Give your best argument for Pluto not having evolved over the years.
2. What year was Pluto discovered?
3. How long does it take Pluto to orbit the Sun?
4. What was Kepler's greatest contribution?

Chapter **10**

Briefing Over: Getting Ready

During the next few months, Jonathan and Ann went through the rigors of astronaut training. Much of their time was spent at the Johnson Space Center and other special facilities throughout the U.S.

They had been able to take advantage of the luxury of special NASA transportation, enjoying the thrill of being flown to the various facilities in T-38 twin jet trainers. This fringe benefit had a purpose.

Practice in the training center (above) is essential for space travel. Below, the water tank prepares astronauts for their weightless experiences in space.

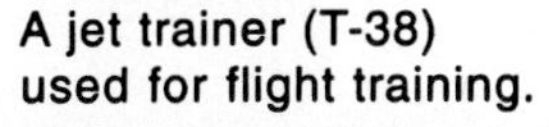

A jet trainer (T-38) used for flight training.

NASA photos

Captain Venture wanted to make sure that Major Paul and Captain Brock kept sharp with their flying skills, and, of course, this was an important part of Jonathan's and Ann's training, as well. The more time they could spend in the air between training periods, the more their bodies and minds would be programmed and put in shape for the strenuous demands of the space-shuttle flight.

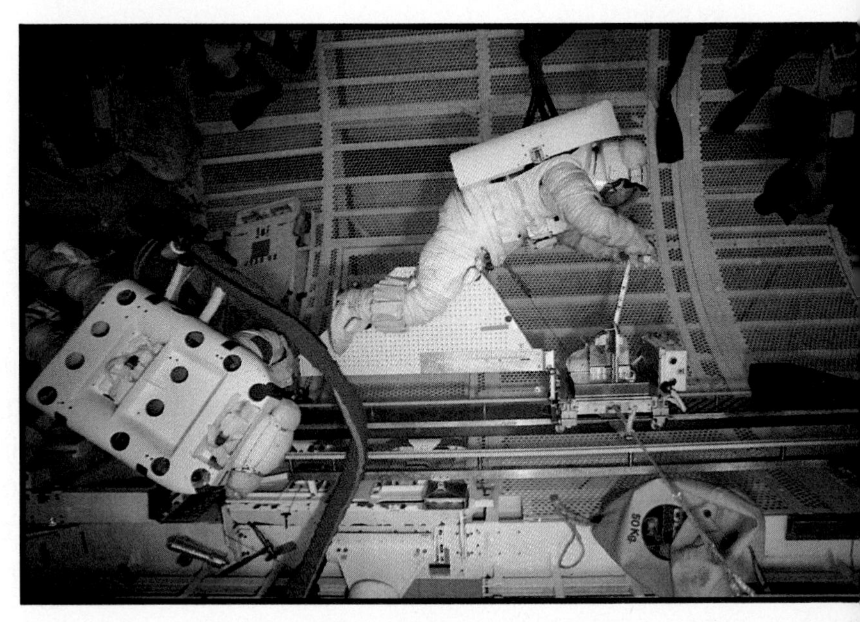

During one of the last days of their rigorous training, Ann, with excitement in her voice exclaimed, "I don't know about you, Jonathan, but I feel ready for our journey to the planets."

"Me too!" commented Jonathan. "After all the training we've had, we should be ready for anything we encounter in space."

"Yes," agreed Ann, "especially since we know we'll be affected by a weightless environment for such a long period of time."

"That's true, Ann, but our training in the deep pool has certainly conditioned us quite well for an extended experience in space."

"Didn't we have fun trying to get the space-walk equipment under control?" quipped Ann.

"Yes," laughed Jonathan. "You looked so funny trying to manage the equipment and yourself, I thought I'd die laughing."

"I looked funny! You should have seen yourself, Mr. Wise Guy!" retorted Ann, trying to look daggers at him, but the picture of Jonathan trying to maneuver in that condition sent her into fits of laughter, and they both ended up laughing so hard people around them looked over and tried to figure out what was so funny.

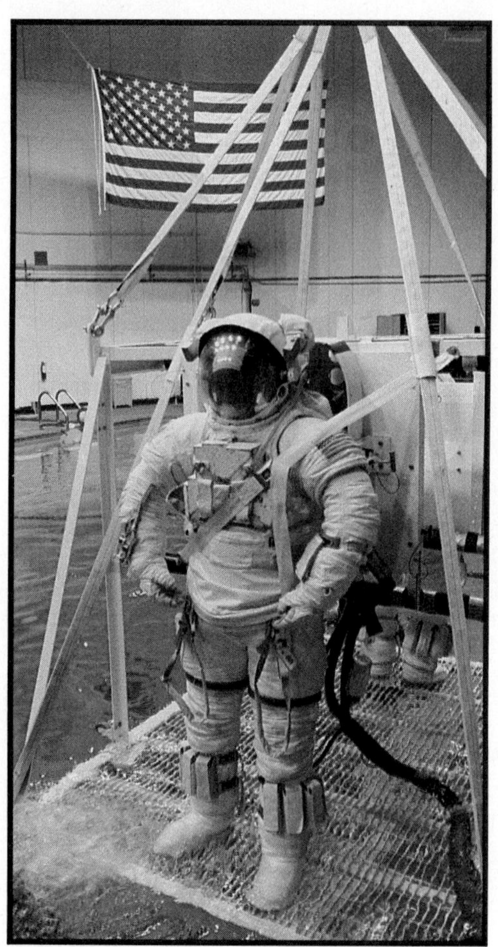

Astronaut getting ready to be lowered into deep-water tank for training. (NASA)

"I guess we won't think it's so funny when we're actually up there trying to operate in that strange environment," said Jonathan seriously, and Ann sobered immediately.

"Yes, I guess you're right," Ann commented. "I have a feeling that both of us are going to get an opportunity to get onto the surface of at least one of the planets."

"No doubt this will be on planet Mars," added Jonathan.

They were both so excited about the coming voyage they couldn't stop talking about it.

"Just think, Jonathan, soon, if everything goes according to schedule, we'll be on our way to the planets!"

It was time for them to hurry into a meeting, where they were met by Captain Venture, along with Captain Brock and Major Paul.

"Well, well, how are you both doing?" the captain asked the young people.

"Fine, Captain," they both answered, and greeted the other two men warmly.

"Well, to get down to business," the captain interrupted, "I've already told you there are some things about this journey that will be classified. One of these areas is our means of propulsion while we're out in space, so I've brought Major Paul and Captain Brock to tell you what they can about this. Major Paul?" The captain gestured for the major to begin the briefing.

"We're going to be faced with a complicated system of propulsion on this voyage," began the major, "using modified rocket boosters and liquid-hydrogen engines as we did on our last voyage.

"At this point, the similarity ends. Our rocket boosters and engines have been changed to give us greater thrust when going from planet to planet. How we've been able to do this is one of those classified aspects of the mission. This new power will enable us to easily reach **Earth's escape velocity** of 25,000 miles per hour, if need be. You'll notice the effects of this additional thrust during blast off, so be aware of it."

Ann and Jonathan looked at each other and shivered with excitement.

Major Paul continued: "Now I want Captain Brock to tell you about a very special development."

Captain Brock started to describe the specialized engines. He pointed out that the Voyager probes traveled at speeds over 32,000 miles per hour. "Our speed will even exceed this," he told them. "These new engine designs will be needed to achieve the super speeds that will be necessary to get from planet to planet. And there's one very important thing that I must mention to you about these engines. They have a nuclear component to them."

"Does this mean radioactivity, Captain?" asked Ann.

"Well, yes, and no," answered the captain. "We'll be perfectly safe, but wherever there is any nuclear activity, we're required to take certain precautions. For example, all of us will be wearing **dosimeters** to check radioactivity. We'll be monitoring these badges throughout the voyage."

"Does this mean there will be certain restricted areas on the shuttle, Captain?" asked Jonathan.

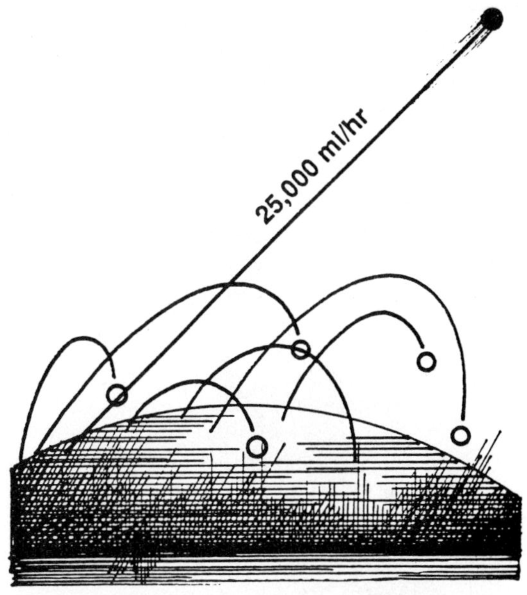

Gas particle escaping the earth's atmosphere after reaching its escape velocity (25,000 mi/hr).

Bullet not arriving at escape velocity returns to Earth.

"No, but it does mean there will be certain areas that must always be considered dangerous, Jonathan," answered Captain Brock.

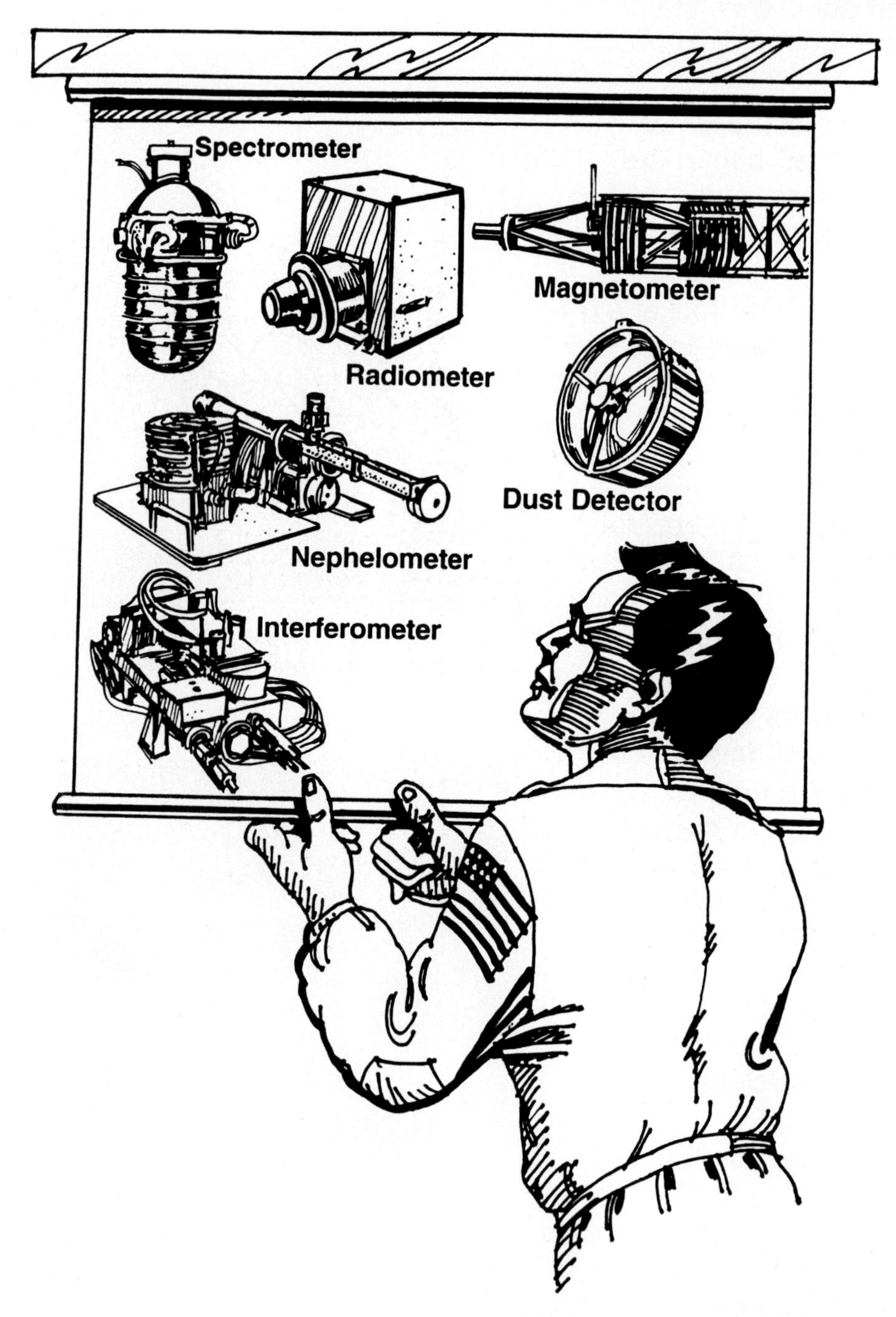

At this point, Major Paul took over again to explain some things about the shuttles' special heat shields and cooling systems. He reminded them that there would be times when the shuttle would be subjected to great extremes of temperature.

Ann leaned over to Jonathan and said, "I know two planets where this will be welcome."

"Yes," exclaimed Jonathan—"Mercury and Venus."

Captain Venture thanked the officers for coming to the briefing. He turned back to Ann and Jonathan, and said, "Now I want to discuss some of the science equipment we'll be using that will enable us to study the planets we'll be visiting."

He walked over to the board and pulled down a screen showing some of the specialized equipment.

"That looks familiar, Captain," spoke up Ann.

"It should," smiled the captain. "This is some of the same equipment we've used on other shuttle missions. Notice this picture of the shuttle equipment we'll be using on the voyage."

“I’ve seen this before, too,” commented Jonathan.

The captain smiled again. “In addition to this, we’ll be stowing a special **lander-type capsule** that will enable us to enter a planet’s atmosphere. We want to get a sample of the gases on these planets.”

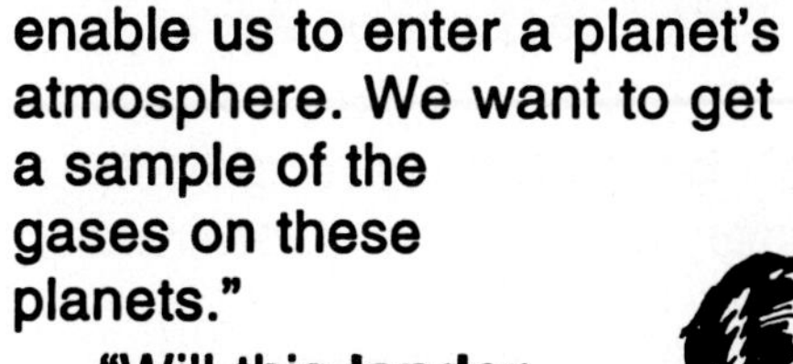

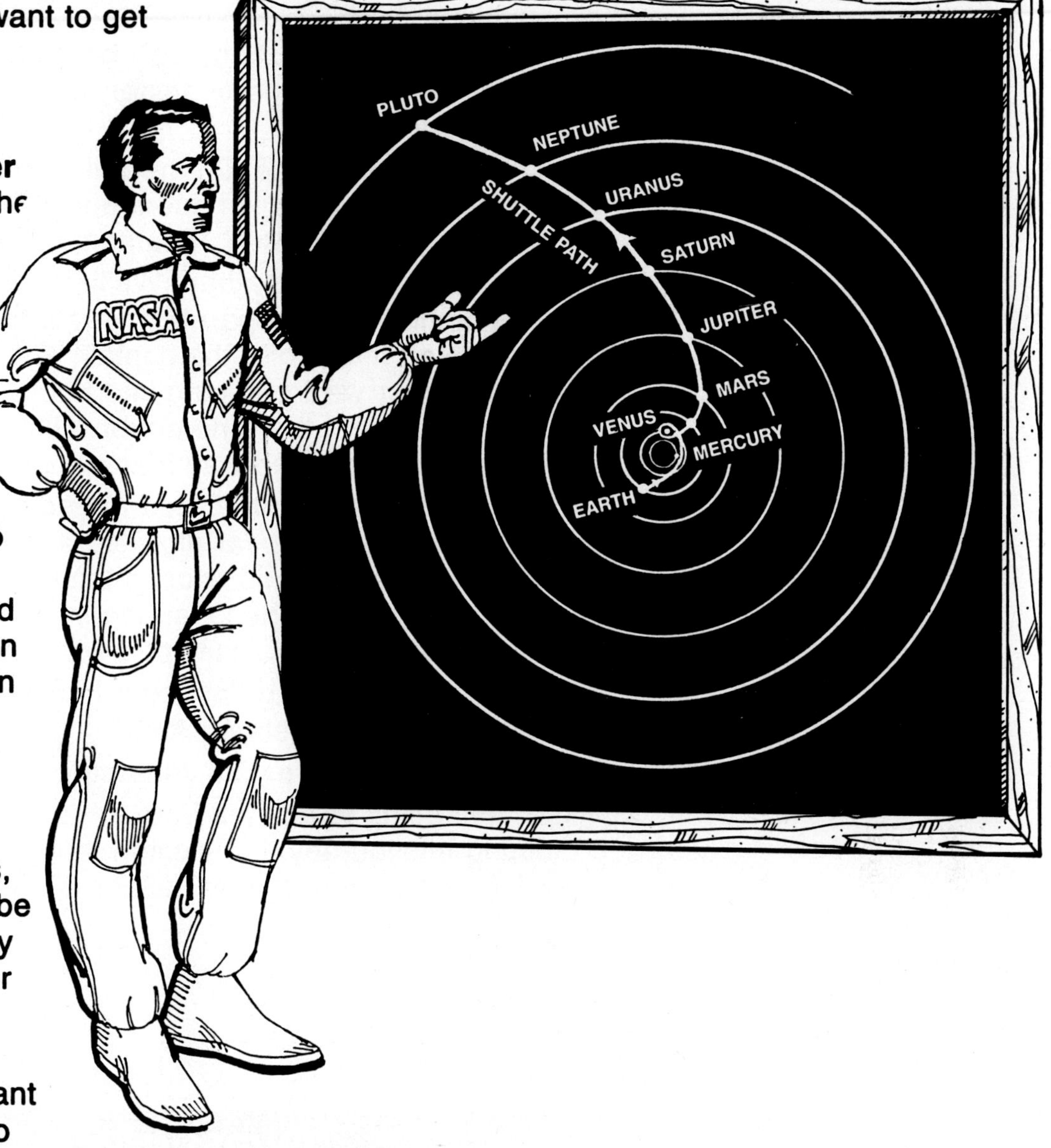

“Will this **lander** allow us to go to the surface of some of the planets, Captain?” asked Jonathan.

“Yes, it will, providing the planet isn’t too hostile. There are special cooling and heating systems on the **lander** that can help us regulate temperature,” answered the captain.

“In other words, Captain, we’ll not be landing on Mercury or Venus, that’s for sure!”

“Not unless you’re cold and want to get warm, or too fat and want to be melted down,” laughed the captain. “You’ll notice that the laboratory deck will be a little different than it was on our last trip. We’ll be doing some chemical analyses on the various samples we take.”

The captain went on to review some of the general procedures that would be used during the flight. Turning to the young people, he announced, “Now for the flight plan!” He unveiled a diagram for the **Voyage to the Planets**.

"As you know, we have a lot of traveling to do, and, fortunately, we have the technology to make this whole trip in about two months."

"That sounds like a long time," responded Ann impatiently.

"But remember, Ann, we'll be very busy, and that will make the time go by faster," smiled the captain at their anxious faces.

"And when we get up there, I'm sure we'll be glad we took all the time we needed to help the trip go smoothly," commented Jonathan wisely.

"That's right, Jonathan. We'll be very glad for all the planning and preparation time it took, when we finally start into orbit," the captain encouraged. "Remember, we'll be going into uncharted territory for humankind, and there no doubt will be more excitement along the way than we planned."

Jonathan and Ann turned to each other and smiled, trying to appear dignified and calm, but it was difficult! They were so excited they could hardly sit there and were ready to launch from their seats right now without the necessity of a spacecraft.

"I know one thing I'm going to pray for during my devotional times," stated Ann.

"What's that?" asked Jonathan.

"I'm going to ask the Lord to protect all of us during this journey. I'm excited, and all that, but there will be new dangers that neither of us has ever faced before."

Questions

1. What special equipment will be used on this voyage?
2. What would you consider the most important inside part of the shuttle on this trip?
3. What is the most important outside part of the shuttle for this trip?
4. Who are the two pilots on this voyage?

Chapter 11

GETTING UNDERWAY

Both Ann and Jonathan knew what to expect; they'd been through this before. They had both spent much time in prayer about this voyage, and they had the faith to believe that not only would they be protected, but that this trip would be profitable and bring them both much joy.

They knew they would be facing dangers, and so, in spite of their faith, they knew they must not be foolish and careless, either.

One of Ann's particular concerns was the **asteroid belt** between Mars and Jupiter.

"I wonder what the probability is that we might get in the way of an **asteroid**," she mentioned to Jonathan.

Jonathan thought a moment. "Well," he answered carefully, "I don't know what the probability is, but I do know there's a lot of space out there, and even though there are thousands of **asteroids** in space from one km to over 300 km in diameter, I think the chances that we'll be struck by one of them is very slight. Remember, Ann, we know where this **belt** is concentrated, so we won't be in the **belt** for very long."

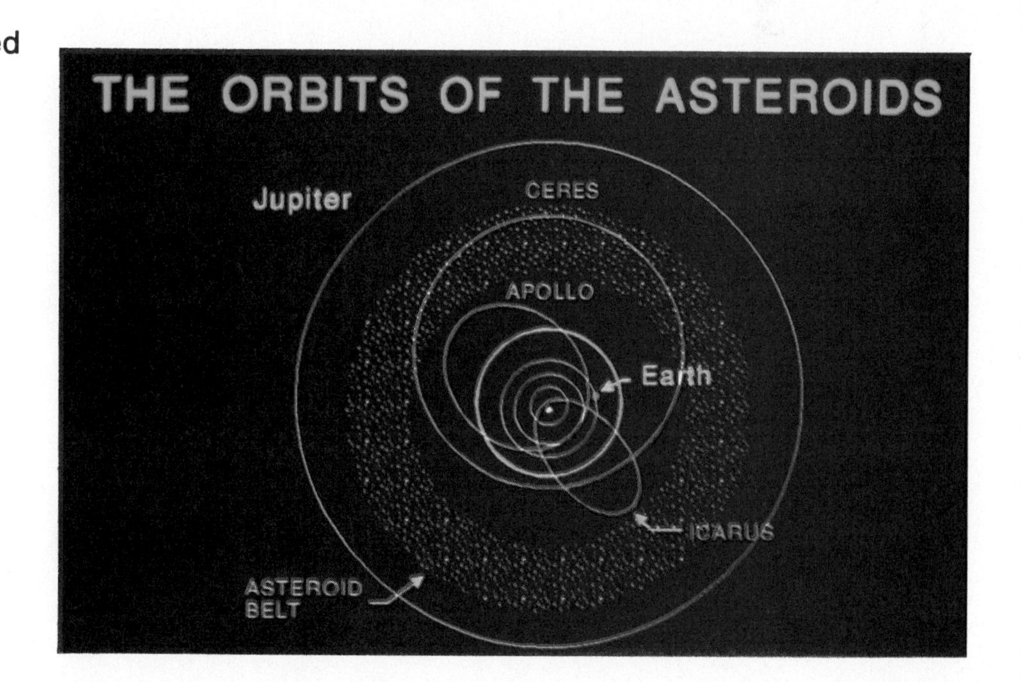

"Well, it's still a bit scary," commented Ann, "even though we feel the Lord is going to protect us in the long run."

So, in spite of their concerns and the long wait to begin their adventure, the day before blast-off finally arrived, and it was time for the young astronauts to get a few hours sleep before they had to suit up.

The early-morning zero hour at 0400 hours was a long time coming, though, for neither of them slept very well. But at last it arrived, and they began the first of many exciting days.

Suiting up for the voyage seemed to go a lot faster this time than it did the previous time they prepared for this. Both of them had little to say to each other while the technicians helped them into their special clothing and double checked the **system connectors** on their space suits.

Ann broke the silence: "Jonathan, somehow this trip to the van seems different than the last one. I wonder what kind of stories we'll have to tell when we come back this time."

"I know one thing," answered Jonathan, "this whole voyage will be exciting! Just the danger alone will be enough to keep us alert the whole time."

NASA astronauts Jack R. Louisma (right), commander, and Gordon Fullerton, pilot, prepare for historic third-orbital-flight test in the Columbia as they walk from a transport van to the launch pad.

Chapter 12

BLAST OFF!

NASA

Time moved very quickly for the young astronauts. It wasn't long before they were on the elevator going up to the top of the spacecraft.

"Three, two, one, ignition!" and then the familiar words, "We have lift off!"

Ann kept up a steady stream of prayer requests to the Lord and Jonathan was going over and over his Bible memory verses. Both of them seemed more intense than they had been on their previous voyage.

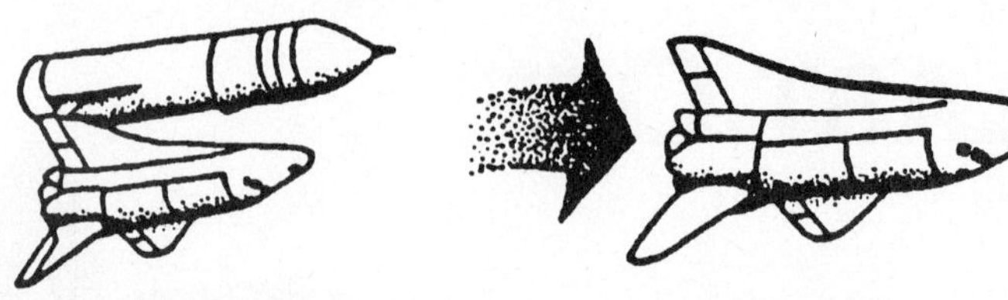

This time, there were more crew members and additional scientists on board. The blast-off routine seemed about the same, except for the feel of the additional thrust they had been told to expect. Major Paul and Captain Brock were intensely monitoring their instruments and talking to Mission Control. That same crackling, fast-paced talk was heard over the communication system.

The familiar **roll maneuver**, beginning at 613 feet, became a reality, and finally the jolt that would kick the spacecraft into the planned 200-mile Earth orbit. Both of them knew they would be doing some orbit time around the earth before they started off to their first stop at planet Mercury.

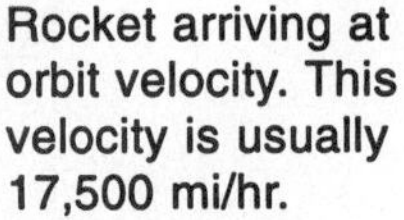

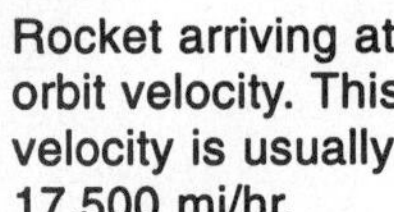

Rocket arriving at orbit velocity. This velocity is usually 17,500 mi/hr.

Questions

1. Why was Ann worried about asteroids?
2. How large can an asteroid be?
3. Where is the large asteroid belt located?
4. How high will the shuttle be when it goes into orbit around planet Earth?

Chapter 13

Good Bye, Planet Earth

NASA

They could feel the weightlessness as they entered orbit. Captain Venture unhooked his seat belt and drifted over to Jonathan and Ann. He opened the conversation to help relax them.

"Well, Kids," he began, "we're in for a once-in-a-lifetime space treat. It's finally a reality that our solar-system trip will be taking us on a 'flyby' past *all* of our planet neighbors. We're going where people have long dreamed of going, but first we'll spend several hours orbiting our own planet."

While Ann was unbuckling her safety belt and getting out of her space suit, she commented, "This will give us a special chance to look down at the earth and take pictures."

"That's right, Ann," the captain said. "You and Jonathan can begin as soon as you get your equipment off. Don't expect to see people or buildings from our 200-mile height, though. Actually, the earth will pass beneath us as a miniature, colorful map."

Jonathan and Ann maneuvered to their windows.

"Look, Jonathan," exclaimed Ann, "look out your window. The earth is beautiful!"

The captain came to stand with them.

"What are those brown streaks on the earth, Captain?" asked Jonathan.

"Hold it," said the captain, "I'll get to all of your questions later, but I have a few questions for you, to start with. What useful pictures do you suppose we can take from Earth orbit, Jonathan?"

Jonathan kept looking out of the window while he answered the captain. "Well, Sir, weather patterns like we see on television might be good to photograph. I'm looking at some very interesting weather going on down there right now. With pictures, people will be able to plan around storms for picnics, or even further rocket launchings."

"That's true," said Ann, "but I was thinking of our creation objectives. Just think, planet Earth has everything in perfect abundance. Just the right amount of oxygen, the right amount of nitrogen, the right amount of carbon dioxide, and Earth is just the right distance from the sun. It seems that we certainly are a special creation."

"Yes," agreed Jonathan, "but that's only part of it. If the earth wasn't tilted 23 1/2 degrees, we wouldn't have any seasons. In fact, the only really comfortable place would be in the mid-latitudes. I'm sure we'll find much more evidence than that before this voyage is over."

"I've seen what are called **infrared space pictures**. Can you explain those, Captain?" asked Ann.

"That's a good question, Ann, and we have that capability with us on this voyage. Actually, **infrared photography** requires a special film that picks up the long red rays of the spectrum, but I'll explain that a little later," the captain said. "But right now, I want to explain the possible value of your own photographs.

"Weather photos are very valuable," he said. "At this moment, you can see entire cloud formations. If you watch, you can follow the movement of large masses of air across the continents. The pictures you take will help in weather prediction. We have weather satellites, of course, and balloons and rockets that are constantly gathering data and reporting the weather you see, and this kind of reporting also can save lives in the case of severe storms."

"I guess this is even more important than I thought," commented Ann.

"Yes, Ann, it's very important. We cannot minimize the importance of weather reporting." The captain went on to explain more about **infrared photography**.

"As I mentioned, **infrared rays** are the *long* rays of the spectrum. These are the rays that are given off by *warm* objects. Knowing this, our special film is sensitive to any change in temperature on the ground. These ground temperatures give off infrared rays, and our special film picks up these rays. The photos are then often color-enhanced with computers."

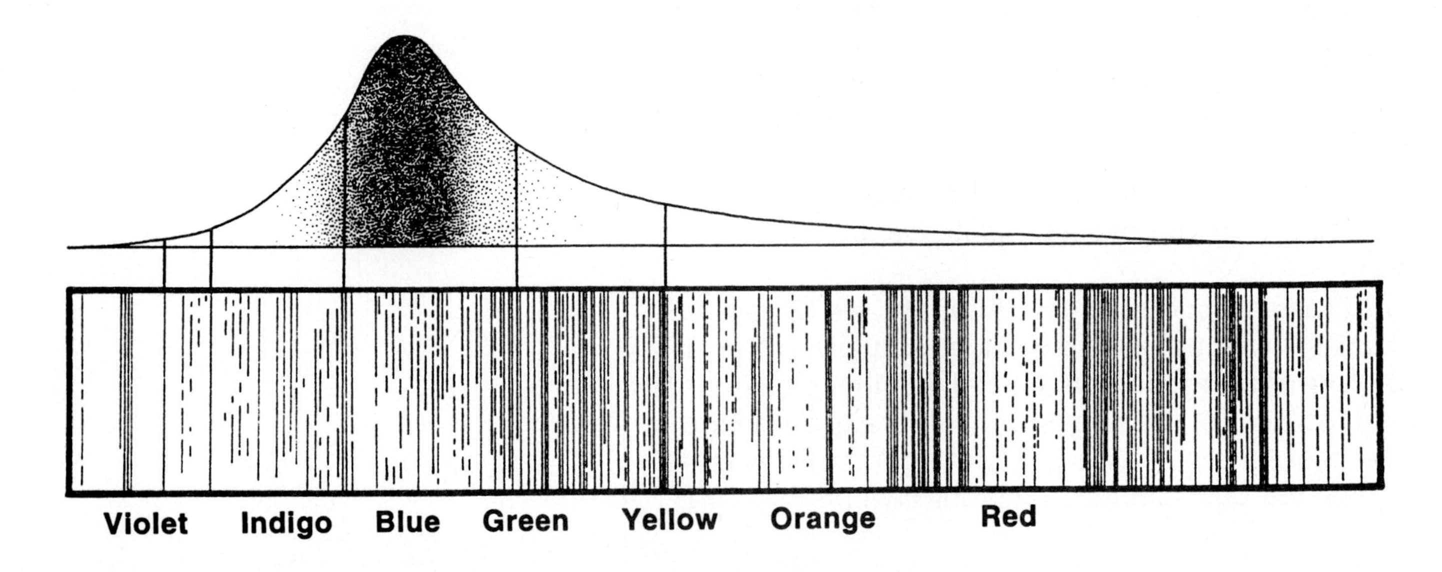

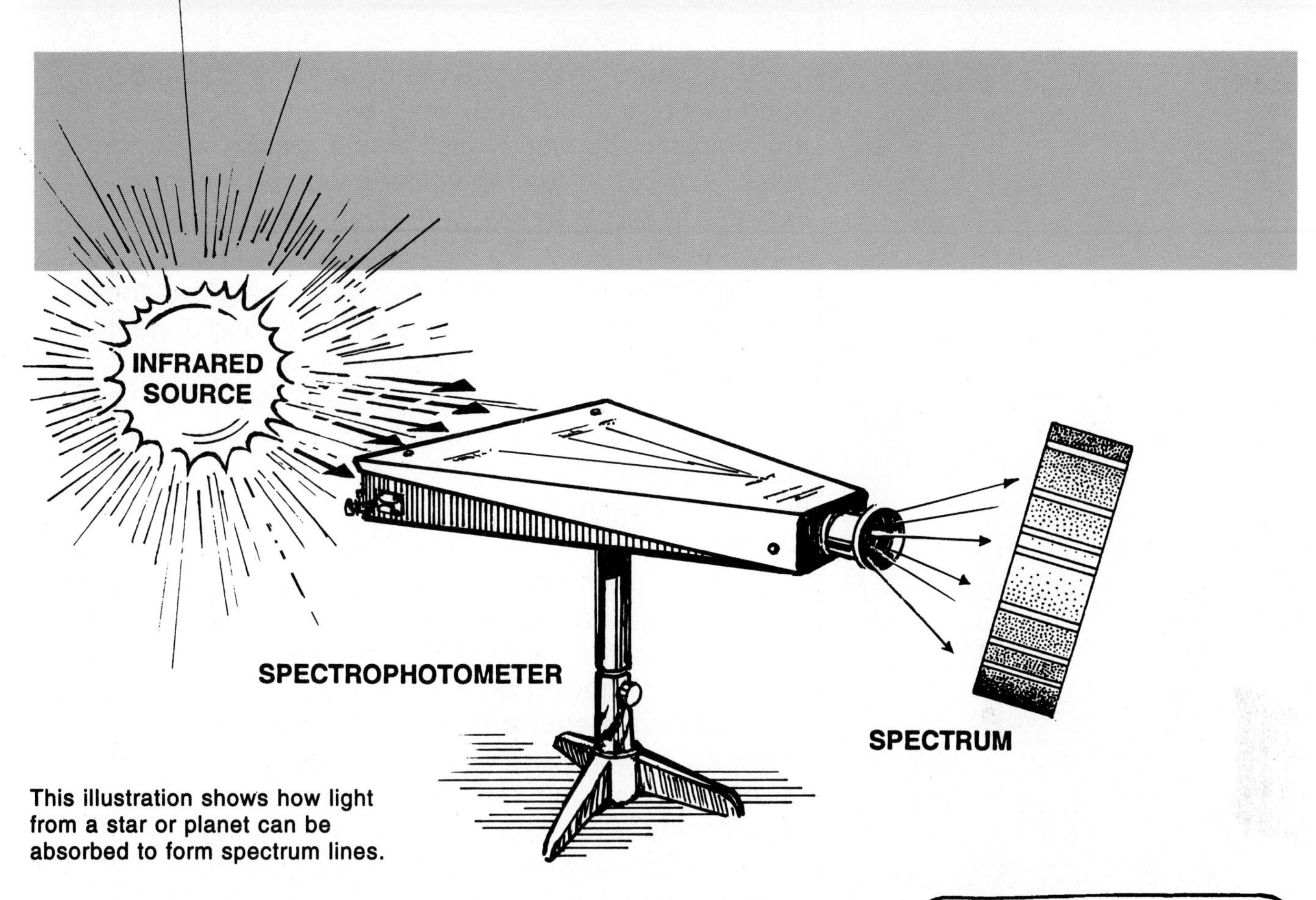

This illustration shows how light from a star or planet can be absorbed to form spectrum lines.

"What do you mean by color-enhanced, Captain?" asked Ann.

"Well," answered the captain, "this is a special computer process. The computer is given a little information, and it then expands that information to make the image clearer."

"Is this something like enlarging a photograph?" questioned Jonathan.

"Yes, that's right. In this case, our film makes different tints of color represent the temperature differences. The computer fine-tunes the film image.

"Just a few uses of the **infrared film** we have on board are to film regions of healthy or diseased vegetation, which can be distinguished easily. This will work especially well with the important rain forests. Also, underground water reserves can be identified, especially in the desert areas. Warm ocean currents, such as the Gulf Stream, can be better understood. And, too, sources of pollution of the air or water can be pinpointed and corrected."

"If a volcano happens to erupt while we're in orbit, will this be of any concern to us?" asked Ann.

"Well, Ann," the captain answered, "there's no need to worry about that! We'll be flying far above any volcanic eruption, which would reach only a few miles, at most. A roaring volcano would look to us like an ant hill far below, with dust spewing out in slow motion."

"So, Captain," Ann said, "we're learning that the usual fears of space are unnecessary," and Jonathan agreed. "Instead, the space age is a marvelous opportunity to look deep into God's creation."

"We've been praying about this voyage for such a long time now," commented Jonathan, "it's hard to believe that we're finally on the first leg of our journey."

By now, the shuttle was full of activity. A steady stream of talk was coming from NASA Control, and the additional members of the crew for this long voyage were moving around the cabin checking their instruments. **Telescopes**, **magnetometers**, **cameras**, **spectroanalyzers**, and many other pieces of laboratory equipment had to be inspected. While experiments were being readied for the long voyage, Captain Venture went over the flight plan with Jonathan and Ann.

"Our decision to orbit planet Earth at least two times will give us an opportunity to check all phases of the shuttle's operation before we leave for planet Mercury. The first planets on our voyage are very rugged bodies, and we'll need to be in perfect shape for this test."

Satellite infrared photo 43 minutes after the eruption of Mount St. Helens. (Courtesy of NOAA)

Questions

1. Make a case for creation from the data in this chapter.
2. What is the tilt of planet Earth's axis?
3. Explain infrared photography in your own words.
4. Will volcanic action on Earth affect us when we are orbiting the earth?

Chapter **14**

HELLO, PLANET MERCURY

The instruments were given a final check along with the various shuttle-cabin details, and the long-awaited report was given to Mission Control. The final okay was given to leave the earth's orbit and continue on to their next destination, Mercury. Everyone in the shuttle was quiet, as Major Paul and Captain Brock positioned the shuttle to leave the earth's orbit. There was a sense of motion as the spacecraft's special thrust mechanism took hold.

Major Paul commented briefly over the intercom: "We're now at **warp speed mode** and heading for planet Mercury."

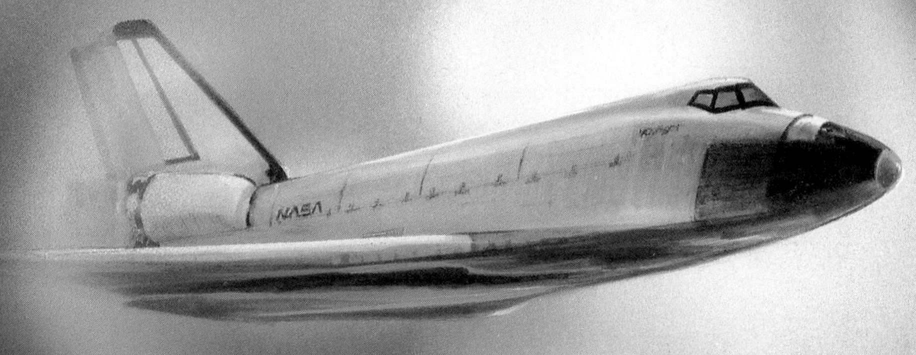

Imaginary warp speed to enable our adventurers to travel quickly through time and space.

Jonathan and Ann were not only quiet, but tense, as they moved at previously unheard-of speeds.

"Jonathan, do you have a strange feeling?" asked Ann. "I don't know how to explain it."

"Yes," answered Jonathan, "it's a strange feeling, all right. I wonder if it's just because we know we're making history with this new mode of travel."

NASA

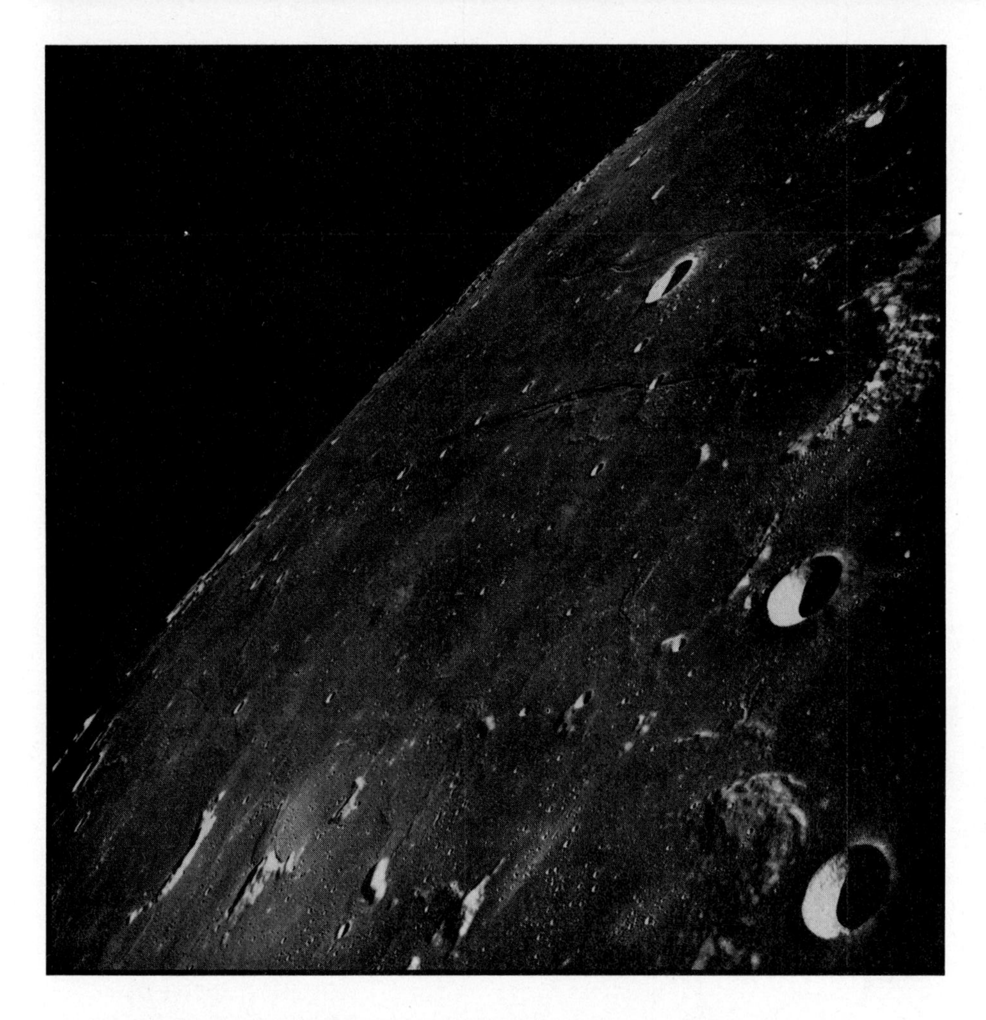

Close-up of Mercury with its lack of atmosphere. (NASA)

It seemed that the short time it took to travel the 90.7 million kilometers to planet Mercury took forever. Even before they got to the planet, they could feel the heat of the sun on the spacecraft. The air-conditioning system was running continuously. Even at maximum, the crew was beginning to perspire.

Captain Venture came over to Jonathan and Ann.

"This is going to be a 'flyby,' so we'll have to collect our samples quickly. Even so, we'll have a good opportunity to view many aspects of the planet," commented the captain. "Look, Kids, we're approaching the planet now."

Ann and Jonathan stood watching it, spellbound!

"It looks so big and full of holes," gasped Jonathan.

"Yes, it looks just like the moon," added Ann.

"That's right, Kids," Captain Venture interrupted, "but notice that there doesn't seem to be much lava-flow evidence at most of the holes."

"Does that mean that the holes had to be caused by meteorites or something, Captain?" asked Jonathan.

"Well, what it means is that those holes *weren't* caused by volcanic action," explained the captain, "and that's about all we can say."

"Doesn't this planet look awesome close up!" Jonathan observed.

"Yes, it does," observed the captain, "and we'd better get moving with our measurements as quickly as we can. This 'flyby' isn't going to last long, and magnetic-field measurements are next on the list."

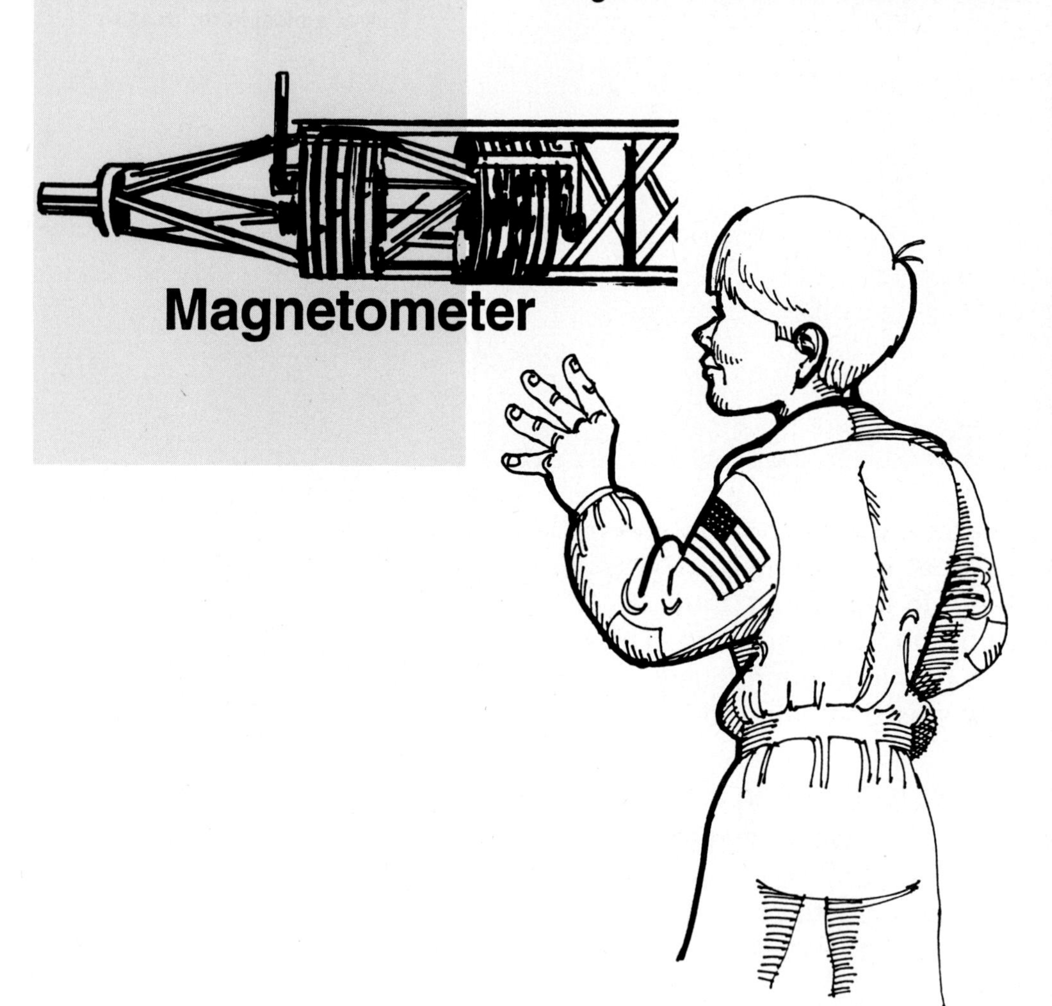

With the **magnetometers** activated, Ann and Jonathan could see the **stylus** showing an increase in the strength of the **magnetic field** around the planet.

"Is this evidence for an iron-rich core in Mercury?" asked Ann.

"Well, it's pretty strong evidence, at this stage, anyway. Look at that **magnetometer stylus** going up."

Jonathan wanted to know if this could mean a high density for the planet.

"It seems that the density of this planet is almost the same as that of planet Earth," the captain answered.

"Captain," Jonathan continued, "does this mean that the mass of the planet is almost the same as the earth's also?"

This drawing gives some idea of how different masses are affected by different amounts of effort (Mass A is greater than Mass B). This same idea applies to the masses of star systems. If they are the same, then the gravitational influence will be the same. If they are different, then the gravitational influence will be different.

"No, remember the charts? Mass and density are quite different in this case. Density is always measured in grams per cubic centimeter. The mass of a planet in our solar system is often measured in relation to the mass of the earth, which is one."

In the meantime, the orbiting shuttle was swinging around planet Mercury on its bright side facing the sun. The outside temperature rose to 430 degrees Centigrade (~806F) and it was going higher.

"I hope the air conditioning holds up," observed Jonathan. "This temperature is beginning to get to me."

"Me, too," added Ann. "How long are we going to be on the sun side of this planet?"

"Not for long," the captain assured them. "We're just about through collecting our data."

Almost as suddenly as the heat came on, the spacecraft seemed to start to cool down. Ann was watching the outside temperature gauge, and it was already down to 200 degrees Centigrade.

Jonathan said he could feel the cabin temperature going down as the spacecraft started to swing around to the dark side of the planet. It wasn't long before the outside temperatures had dropped to almost minus 170 degrees Centigrade (-280 degrees Fahrenheit). Now the spacecraft was fighting off the freezing temperatures of the dark side of the planet.

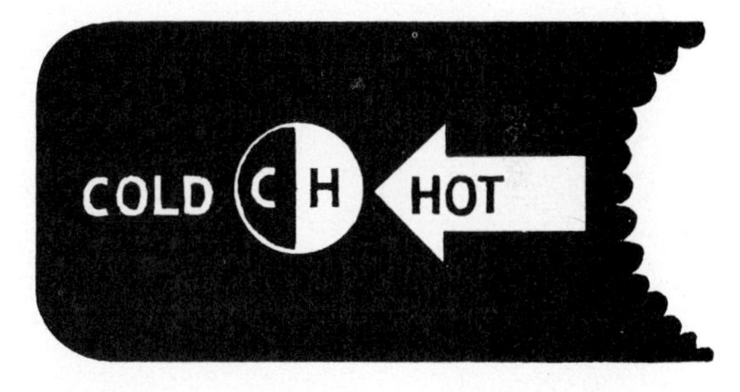

This diagram shows how planet Mercury can get so hot on one side and so cold on the other.

Spectrometer

This compact spectrometer is used in the analysis of solar objects from satellites and shuttles.

"I didn't think I'd ever see temperatures change so fast," commented Jonathan.

But Ann was interested in another aspect of the operation at the moment. "What kind of surface data are we receiving so far, Captain?"

"Well," the captain replied, "the **spectroanalyzers** are showing oxygen, sodium, helium, hydrogen, and even a little dust."

"And isn't that just about what we expected?"

"Yes, it is Ann, but this is the scientific truth we've been looking for."

"So it looks like we're getting pretty accurate data so far," observed Jonathan. "Is Venus going to be a 'flyby' also, Captain?"

"I can't say for sure at this moment, Jonathan. We're just going to have to wait a little longer before we make that decision. If we can collect enough scientific data in a 'flyby,' then so much the better!"

Just then Captain Brock's voice broke in over the intercom. "Get ready for **warp speed mode**. We're now heading for planet Venus. We have a 50-million-kilometer trip ahead of us this time. Secure all equipment and fasten your restraining belts."

Questions

1. What testimony does Mercury give for a creator and against evolution?
2. Describe the atmosphere of Mercury in your own words.
3. What do you think caused the temperature differences on planet Mercury?
4. Where would you look for Mercury in the sky?

Chapter 15

VENUS: THE HOT PLANET

Suddenly the cabin grew quiet. Everyone felt the jolt as the special engines kicked in. Once again the spacecraft zipped through space at an incredible speed, and Jonathan and Ann watched in amazement as their spacecraft left planet Mercury.

Ann broke the silence. "I can't believe we're seeing God's creation in space firsthand."

"I know," answered Jonathan. "I've been thinking of God's comments in the Bible about the heavens being the work of His fingers."

The spacecraft was almost an hour into its flight when Major Paul's voice was heard over the intercom. "Prepare for **retro slowdown**. Be sure all equipment is secure."

As they watched, both Jonathan and Ann saw the planet Venus come into view.

"Jonathan, look at that! I can't believe what I'm seeing!"

"I know," answered Jonathan, "this is beyond belief. Look at that cloud layer! It seems to cover the whole planet!"

Showing Venus with its dense cloud cover of water, sulfuric acid, and other caustic substances. NASA)

"You haven't seen anything yet, Kids," the Captain broke in. "Wait until we get to some of the other planets. Hurry and finish your work. We'll not be staying around Venus for very long. We'll take one loop around the planet and then sling-shot our way to Mars."

"Why such a short stay for Venus, Captain?" asked Ann. "I thought we had a lot of data to collect here?"

"That's precisely why we aren't going to stay in the area long. Our analysis so far is worse than we expected. The temperature under those clouds is already reading over 470 degrees Centigrade and that's only half the problem."

"I remember studying something about sulfuric and hydrochloric acids in the Venus atmosphere," commented Jonathan.

"You're right, Jonathan. This planet is loaded with carbon dioxide, which, as you well know, contributes to its extremely hot temperature. But it's the acids that worry us. We're recording droplets of sulfuric acid in some of that cloud vapor, and we can only guess at what that would do to some of the external structures of our spacecraft. We need to get out of here as quickly as we can," the captain stated.

"And that seems so strange," commented Jonathan, "because this planet almost looks as though there could be life on it. And now, here we are, close enough to make a careful analysis of it, and we find it's too dangerous a planet."

"And this is the hottest planet in the solar system," added Ann, "which makes it a very frightening planet, as well. It also has the reputation of being the rockiest planet in the universe, too. According to our **X-ray** and **Doppler analysis** of the surface, it doesn't look very pleasant."

The captain had left to answer a call on the intercom, but now he was moving back over to them. "Well, we have all the data we're going to get on this 'flyby,' so let's secure and brace ourselves for a long trip. According to the original flight plan, we're on our way to a 119-plus million-kilometer trip to Mars."

Questions

1. Make your best case for a creator, after viewing Venus.
2. What seems to be the cause of the great Venus temperature?
3. In your opinion, what is the greatest danger for humans on planet Venus?
4. Describe the surface of Venus. How do we get information from under the Venus atmosphere?

Chapter 16

MARS: A PERSONAL VISIT TO THE PLANET

The young astronauts really were excited about this. They knew they might get to the surface on *some* of the planets, and *Mars* might be the best candidate for that experience.

Jonathan turned to the captain. "Does this mean a possible landing on Mars?"

The captain smiled. "Well, anything's possible, Jonathan. If things look good, we're going to have a go at it!"

They couldn't believe what they were hearing; they could hardly wait.

Captain Venture kept briefing Ann and Jonathan on their way, and then the familiar voice of Major Paul was heard again over the intercom: "Get ready for **retro slowdown** to establish a Mars' orbit."

It wasn't long before they had established their orbit around the planet. Preparation to put the **lander module** in operation began almost immediately. It didn't take the young astronauts long to get into their space suits. They were ready for an exciting adventure on the planet Mars.

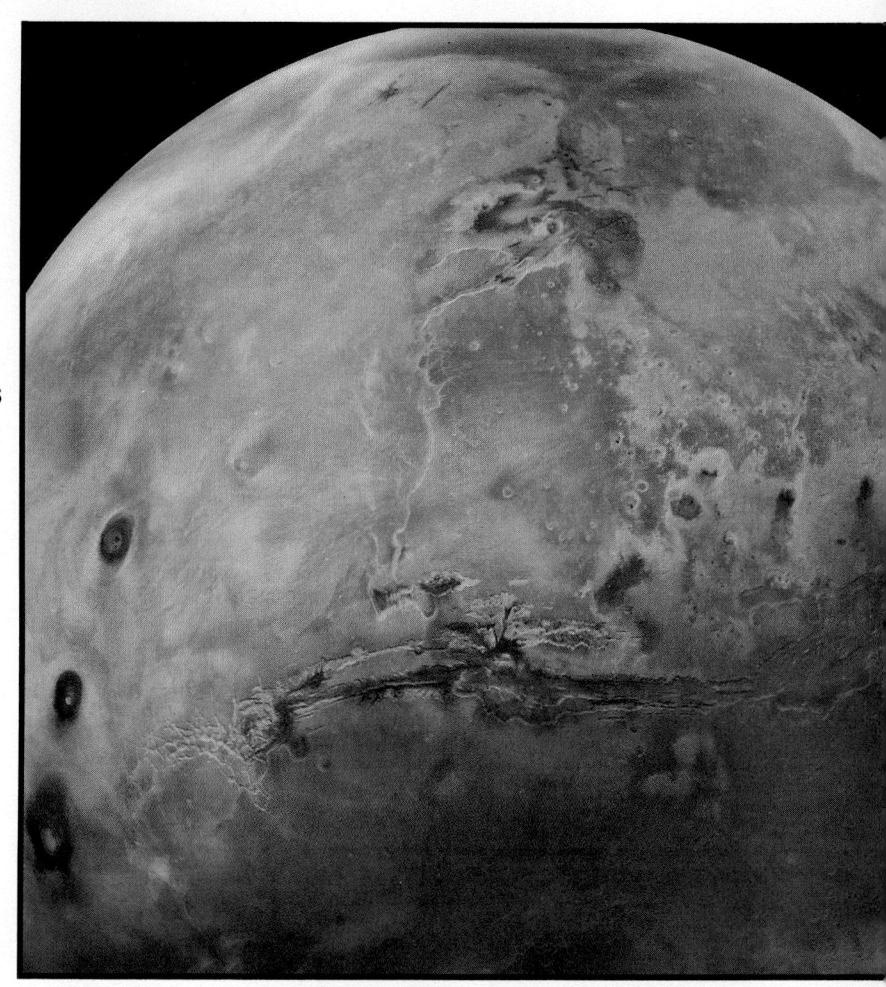

Mars is the one planet that has offered the greatest hope for finding life. None has been found. (NASA)

Upon command, the Captain, Ann, and Jonathan scrambled into the compact **lander**. This was the vehicle that would take them to the surface of Mars, and Ann and Jonathan had mixed emotions about it. They were excited, of course, but they also were a little apprehensive. So many things could go wrong, but they remembered their months of preparation and the praying they had done about this trip, and their

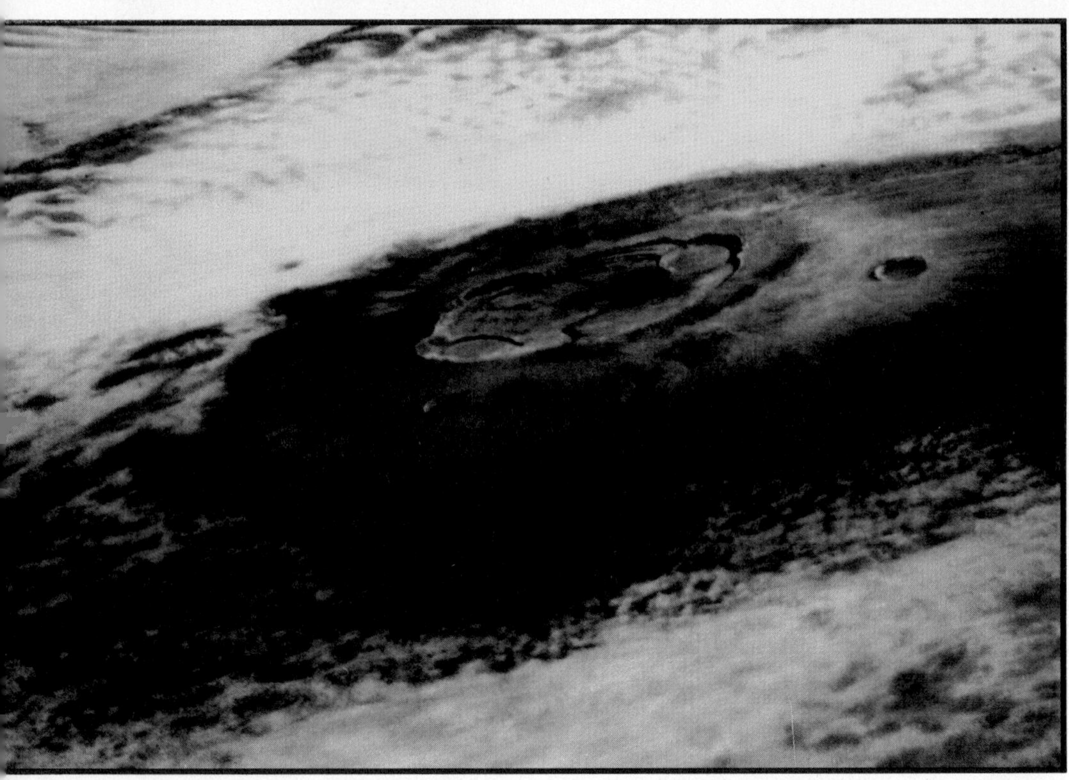

NASA

This photo of Olympus Mons (great volcano) gives some idea of its awesomeness. The mountain measures nearly 2,000 miles around (3,221 km) at its base.

faith in God's protecting power helped keep them calm and alert.

Captain Venture seemed to be very calm on the outside, but Jonathan and Ann could tell that this was a very special moment for him, also.

The **lander** slowly raised itself out of the cargo bay and then gradually started its descent toward Mars. Down they dropped toward the sandy surface, slowed by small, steering, rocket engines and a large parachute. The **special sensors** on board the **lander** were reading the **atmospheric contents** as it descended.

"Just as we expected," the captain observed, "carbon dioxide, ozone, argon, and a hint of carbon monoxide."

Suddenly the **lander** thumped and became very quiet! They were finally on the surface of Mars!

Jonathan wasn't aware that in his excitement he had been holding his breath, and when he realized they were finally down, he began breathing again, with relief.

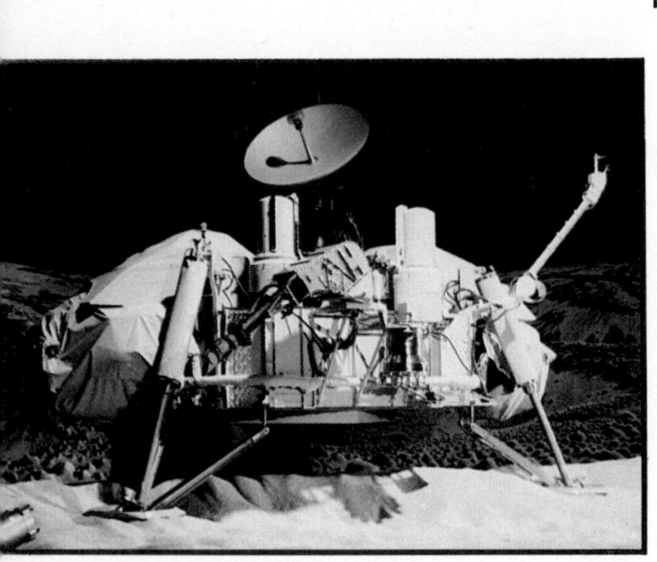

Viking Lander (NASA)

After checking their space suits, the door opened to a bright, rocky landscape. Climbing out, Jonathan,

Ann, and the Captain noticed that their weight was considerably less than on Earth.

The first landing of any spacecraft on Mars. The arms used in the experiments are in close view. No evidence of life was found. (NASA)

"My!" quipped Ann, "I wish I'd thought to bring along a box of cream puffs and a chocolate cake. I could eat those up here without feeling guilty."

The captain laughed. "I don't think you have much of a problem about that even on Earth, Ann, so I'll make a promise to you. When we get back to Earth I'll buy you a chocolate cake and a big box of cream puffs."

"Hey, what about me?" asked Jonathan, "I like chocolate cake and cream puffs, too!"

The captain laughed again. "Well, I guess I can find a bakery with enough of them to satisfy the both of you," he retorted.

As they walked away from the **lander**, Ann exclaimed, "Seriously, though, this is like walking and floating in deep water except that there's no water to slow us down!"

"Mars' gravity is 60 percent less than Earth's," explained the captain, "so be careful how you move around. You could get hurt or tear your space suits, and that would mean serious trouble!"

The three astronauts spread out and began collecting sand-and-rock samples and putting them into their sterile bags, just as they had been instructed. After stowing them on the **lander**, the three then ventured off to do some more exploring. They were wise enough to keep the **lander** in sight. This was certainly not a time to get lost.

They took pictures of deep craters, giant canyons, and dormant volcanoes. It was a desert wonderland! Every place was completely dry. There were no lakes, no rivers, no rain, nor waterfalls in their viewing range.

Jonathan called to the others over the intercom. "This is an interesting place, all right, but it's so barren and rocky!"

"That's right," replied the captain, "and, as we expected, there obviously doesn't seem to be any other life around here." They were silent for a moment, each thinking their own thoughts. The captain broke the silence by pondering, "In my own opinion, nothing could ever have evolved on *this* planet. Our Creator must have made planet Mars in an instant of time."

"He apparently chose not to make any Martians here, that's for certain," quipped Jonathan.

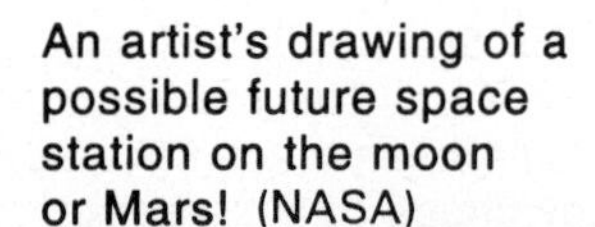

An artist's drawing of a possible future space station on the moon or Mars! (NASA)

Astronauts brace themselves for the fierce storms that frequently occur on planet Mars. They need to get out of the path in a hurry. (NASA)

Ann looked up. "This strange sky! It's so awesome it scares me! Instead of a blue sky with clouds, it's a pink color. And look at that spooky darkness in the distance. It almost looks like it's coming toward us."

In an instant the captain was on the alert. "It's time to get out of here," the captain shouted suddenly, trying to keep the alarm out of his voice. "There's a dust storm approaching! Look over there at that big mountain."

"You mean over there to our right?" asked Ann.

"Yes. That's Olympus Mons and over there is Valles Marineris, and we'd better get out of here in a hurry."

They maneuvered as quickly back to the **lander** as their **space suits** would allow and scrambled aboard. Mission Control ordered an immediate departure from planet Mars and the **lander** blasted off from the weak gravitational field and started back to the shuttle, which was faithfully circling the planet.

They had blasted off just as the dust storm broke upon Mars, and they all breathed a sigh of relief.

Mission Control had been anxiously awaiting their return to the shuttle, and as soon as they were on board the spacecraft again, Captain Venture ordered the gear and samples stowed, coordinating their orbital exit instructions with Ann and Jonathan, waiting for Mission Control instructions. Mission Control wasted no time giving them the go ahead.

"Boy!" quipped Ann when she could get herself calmed down a bit, "I've hurried into a building before to get out of a rain or snow storm, but the fleeing—or trying to flee—from this storm isn't one I want to experience again very soon."

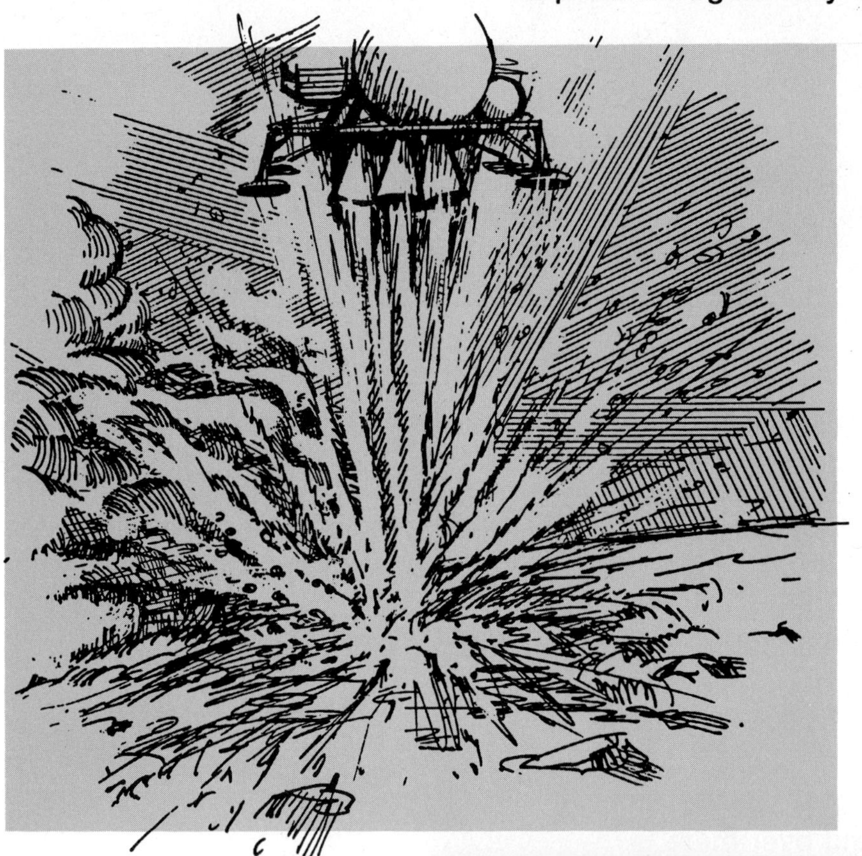

"Yes," agreed Jonathan as he removed his space suit, "it was kind of scary, wasn't it! If I'm going to get lost, I'd like it to be a little closer to home, like in the mountains facing an angry bear or a pack of wolves. That just couldn't be as frightening as this was!"

"If we had remained on Mars," the captain continued seriously, "we might have lost our direction in all that dust and would have had to remain there for a long, long time."

Questions

1. Using planet Mars for the example, give your best case for creation.
2. Describe the Mars atmosphere in your own words.
3. Describe the surface of Mars in your own words.
4. Name one significant mountain on Mars.

Chapter 17

THAT'S REALLY JUPITER!!!

The outward journey next took the explorers through the **asteroid belt** between Mars and Jupiter. They took spectacular pictures of the **asteroids**. The shuttle technicians collected dust samples as they zoomed toward Jupiter.

Thankfully, there was no collision, but there was no opportunity to land on an asteroid, either. These giant rocks, some of them as big as mountains, were spread out thinly, and none of them came very close to the shuttle.

Within hours, giant Jupiter loomed through the shuttle windows and appeared as a giant gas ball, similar to the sun. It seemed to grow larger by the minute!

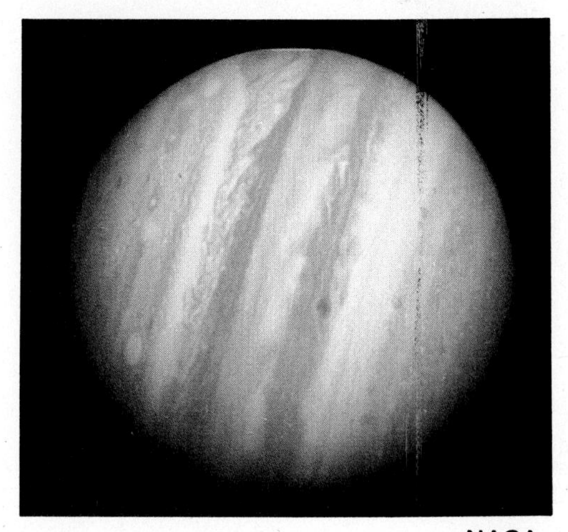

NASA

"Will we be able to land on Jupiter and collect samples, Captain?" asked Ann.

"Ann," exclaimed Jonathan in surprise, "you've forgotten your lesson."

Ann looked sheepish. "That *was* silly of me, wasn't it?"

The captain laughed and tried to reassure her. "Don't feel embarrassed, Ann. This journey has been so exciting I'm not surprised you'd forget. But remember that Jupiter has no place to land, because we'd fall into it and never get out. This planet is just a giant gas ball."

"I've heard that some astronomers call Jupiter the 'King of the Solar System,'" remarked Jonathan.

"Right," answered the captain. "It's more massive than all the other planets combined. We'll make observations as we do a 'flyby' along the way, but remember that Jupiter has intense radiation and poisonous gases."

The captain pointed out the window suddenly and spoke excitedly: "Look at the red spot below us. That's a giant, swirling hurricane!"

NASA

They all watched in awe for some time. The young astronauts could see many of Jupiter's moons, which showed a great variety of colors and markings. The Moon **Io** was especially pretty, being red-orange in color and having active volcanoes.

Jupiter and its four major moons, combined in a composite picture. (NASA)

"It looks like a scoop of orange sherbet," said Jonathan. "Why is that, Captain?"

"Well," the captain answered, "our instruments show that **Io** is covered with sulfur compounds, which often appear red or yellow.

"This makes each of the moons of Jupiter unique and colorful. I'm sure they'll continue to be a problem for the evolutionists' theory that the solar system formed naturally. There is simply too much variety in them for any single origin theory to explain, except when we realize they were created by a Master Designer, who alone could create them."

"I'm sure glad I know enough to believe the Bible and realize that God created all this," smiled Ann. "And it certainly makes more sense when we look at the scientific data."

"How right you are, Ann," agreed Jonathan. "Without the Creator, you don't have much of anything going for you on this or any other issue."

"You're certainly both right about that," smiled the captain. "This trip continues to show evidence of the Creator in every direction we look. From what we're seeing, I don't think we have to be afraid of scientific data disproving the Bible. It's simply not going to be able to do it! Scientific discovery seems to support a Creator and Master Designer as the first cause."

"God is certainly the Artist with all of this color," added Jonathan. "Who would ever have thought of an orange-colored, sulfur-covered moon except the Creator Himself?"

Questions

1. Make your best case for creation from your observations of Jupiter.
2. Explain, in your own words, why you would not want to land on Jupiter.
3. Describe the atmosphere of Jupiter in your own words.
4. How many moons does Jupiter have? Name the most exciting one, and tell why it is so.

Chapter 18

LOOK OUT, SATURN— HERE WE COME!

Once again they recognized the voice of Major Paul coming over the intercom, urging them to hastily fasten their security belts and to prepare for **warp speed mode** once again.

After the next rapid leap, at super speeds across the empty space, the travelers passed above the magnificent planet Saturn. Just as with Jupiter, Saturn was not solid, and there was no place to land.

"Look at those rings!" shouted Ann. "They're so much larger than what we saw in our telescopes back home."

Color-enhanced picture of Saturn showing its beauty from a distance. (NASA)

"They're surely big enough for a skateboard," quipped Jonathan.

"Or even a million of them," laughed Ann. "They seem to be just thin layers of rocks and ice crystals, though."

As they drew even nearer, they soon noticed more details on the rings. "Just as I thought," spoke up the captain. "The rings show braids, knots, and different colors, the same as the **Voyager probes** indicated a few years ago.

"This may show that Saturn's rings have not had billions of years to combine and spread out with each other, and, if this is true, it's another problem for the evolutionists. Anyway, we'll capture all these ring

A close-up of the multiple rings of Saturn. (NASA)

details with our **high-resolution cameras** for later study."

"I see what you mean," responded Ann. "If appearance means anything, the solar system is a young one. I think this certainly looks like the universe was created just a few thousand years ago."

"Yes," agreed Jonathan, "and here it all is before us, still looking fresh and new. I'm glad God allowed me the privilege of making this voyage and seeing this for myself. And I'm glad He allowed you and Ann to share in this adventure, too, Captain," he replied as an afterthought.

"Well, thanks, Jonathan. I'm glad we could too," smiled the captain.

They continued on their journey, and hours later the gaseous planets Uranus and Neptune came into view outside their windows. The astronauts didn't even want to sleep or even take their eyes off the windows. This space show was simply too good to miss—the chance of a lifetime!

Questions

1. Make your best case for creation based upon your observations of planet Saturn.
2. What do Saturn's rings seem to be made of?
3. What significant thing about Saturn's rings is important to consider in its origin?
4. Saturn is called one of a group of four special planets. What are these planets called?

Chapter 19

ON TO URANUS

A call from the flight deck for **retro slowdown**, and the majesty of planet Uranus loomed before them. As the spacecraft came closer, Ann's excitement became evident.

"Look, Captain and Jonathan, you can see one of its moons."

The captain and Jonathan left the equipment they were working on and scrambled to the window.

Uranus is a cold planet with 15 known moons. The most noteworthy of the moons are: Ariel, Miranda, and Umbriel.

"That must be **Ariel**," explained the captain. "If you look down at the lower left corner and to the side, you'll see **Miranda**, the smallest and strangest of Uranus' moons. There's **Umbriel**, too. That's the only one of the moons that doesn't seem to have any volcanic activity on it. I'm sure you remember that we said Uranus had five moons. Now I have to tell you that Voyager discovered ten additional moons."

"In other words, we should always be ready for new information and not be dogmatic about our beliefs," replied Jonathan.

"That's exactly what I want to teach you," added the captain.

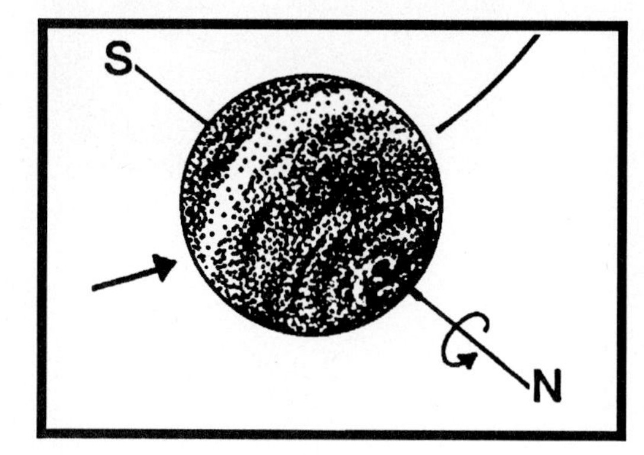

Thinking of his and Ann's hours of study and research, Jonathan added, "but I never thought we'd actually be looking at them."

"Just think," Ann commented, "that planet is spinning in a different direction than most of the other planets. Doesn't it seem as though it was placed there as a special testimony to its Creator?"

"Well," laughed Jonathan, "it sure complicates any idea that all of the planets came from a single ball of gas and dust, doesn't it?"

"It also makes you think of the awesomeness of planetary space," added the captain. "Scientists are confused about what they are seeing in the planets. Every time we think we know something, we find we didn't know it after all, when we finally get out there."

Taking an even closer look, Ann commented, "Look! Isn't it amazing how sharp the Uranus rings are?"

NASA

"Yes," agreed the captain, "they're very sharp, and that's one of the problems the evolutionists have to face. They're only about ten miles wide, and most scientists agree that they must have been formed quite recently."

"The scientific evidence for a recent creation seems to be getting stronger as we go along, huh Jonathan?" observed Ann.

Just about that time Captain Brock broke in on them over the intercom. "Secure for **warp speed mode**. We're off to Neptune!"

Questions

1. What evidence for creation can you give by viewing planet Uranus?
2. How wide are the rings of Uranus? What significance is this for creation?
3. How many moons does Uranus have?
4. Describe the rotation of Uranus on its axis.

Chapter 20

OFF TO NEPTUNE!!

The flight crew was busy with their navigating. Any slight nudge in empty space could throw the spacecraft off their target, and they had to be very, very careful. This was especially true in the outer regions of space.

It was quite dark this far out from the sun, and both Ann and Jonathan commented that the planets looked like giant basketballs, slowly moving through the empty darkness. The distant sun seemed small, too, like a bright star.

Neptune with one of its satellites. (NASA)

All of a sudden Neptune loomed into view and seemed to be sitting there like a lonely ball.

Suddenly, Captain Venture shouted excitedly. "There's the new moon," he exclaimed. "See, there's **Triton** and **Nereid**, and over there is Moon 1989N1."

Showing Proteus, the newest in Neptune's family. (NASA)

"Why in the world did they name it 1989N1, Captain?" asked Ann.

"Well, Ann, **Voyager** had just found it, and the astronomers hadn't had a chance to name it yet. I want to report now, though, that they have decided on a name for it. You can now call it **'Proteus'**."

"I suppose they want to be careful and give it a proper name," spoke up Jonathan.

The captain explained to Jonathan and Ann that here was a planet that was giving off more heat than it was getting from the sun, according to the sensors.

"Captain, do you mean that Neptune is giving off heat even when its surface temperature is minus 214 degrees Celsius?"

"That's what our sensors are saying here on board, Ann," said the captain. "Let's be cautious though. I seem to recall from our flyby that both Jupiter and Saturn were doing the same thing. If so, this is good evidence that they can't be very old."

Ann quickly went through the Jupiter and Saturn data. "You're right captain. See here? We did get that kind of reading from the sensors. They aren't as dramatic as Neptune seems to be though."

Jonathan continued to look at the dials and a computer print-out sheet for confirmation. This was another short "flyby," so it wasn't long before the familiar voice of Major Paul was heard, telling them to secure for their next destination.

"Aye, aye, Sir," called back Ann. "Pluto! Here we come!"

Questions

1. How does Neptune testify of creation?
2. Describe the Sun as it would be observed from Neptune.
3. What is the name of the newest Neptune moon?
4. Describe the importance of the heat that is given off of planet Neptune.

Chapter 21

ON TO PLUTO

Finally, it was Pluto's turn for inspection!

"Do you realize that we're now four billion miles outward from Earth?" asked the captain. "Without our superspeed engines, we never could have made it. At 100 miles per hour, it would take 4,500 years to reach Pluto, and Pluto is seventy-five times farther from the earth than Mars at the present time."

"I'm glad we speeded up this trip," quipped Ann. "Otherwise it would be rather difficult for humans to take a trip that long."

"Yes," grinned Jonathan, "and we'd never get our chocolate cake and cream puffs, either."

The captain laughed. He was pleased to see that their sense of humor hadn't diminished, in spite of their excitement and anxieties.

The shuttle heaters ran constantly now. Pluto's surface temperature was measured by **probes** to be minus 218 degrees Celsius. Instruments indicated that there was no oxygen to breathe on Pluto, and that only a thin layer of methane frost was on the surface. The crew quickly agreed that Pluto would not be a safe place to land.

"Oh," sounded Jonathan disappointedly, "I was hoping we could go hiking on Pluto and ski down the frozen hills!"

"Well," laughed the captain, "this is a scientific mission for gathering data, and we must remember our objective."

"Look there," said Ann, pointing to the radiation sensors, "according to these sensors, the sun's radiation is more than 1500 times less than it is on Earth."

"Yes, I've been watching that," stated the captain. "I guess this is just another bit of evidence for Earth's uniqueness, because God certainly didn't equip *this* planet for anything to live on it."

Newton can feel the cold that Pluto probes have found to be minus 218°C.

Radiometer

This is a very sensitive instrument that will detect heat radiation coming from an object such as a planet.

"Where did Pluto get its name, Captain?" asked Ann.

"It was named shortly after its discovery back in 1930," explained the captain. "Pluto was the god of the underworld in Greek mythology. I'm sorry that God's planets always seem to be named after false gods like this. But it doesn't really matter, when you think about it, because we know it was the *true* God who made these majestic planets. Incidentally, the Disney cartoon dog, Pluto, was also named the very same year, in 1930. It must have been a popular name that year!"

"Pluto doesn't look at all like its neighbors, does it?" observed Jonathan. "It's so small and seems to be a mixture of rock and ice."

Artist's conception of approach to Pluto as Ann and Jonathan may have viewed it.

"That's correct, Jonathan," answered the captain. "It definitely appears to be out of place among the gas giants like **Uranus** and **Neptune**."

"Maybe the Creator put Pluto here to make us *wonder*," said Ann almost to herself.

"What do you mean, Ann?" asked Jonathan with a puzzled expression.

"Well, we found that the solar system certainly is filled with *wonder*. I mean, we can enjoy all the colorful and complicated things, but we can't explain them. Maybe Pluto was added to show us that there is no end to the variety of objects in space. And there may be even more planets out beyond Pluto that we don't know about yet."

The captain listened to their discussion quietly. He was satisfied that Jonathan and Ann were thinking hard. He silently thanked the Lord for a new generation of young people who were able to fit the Lord's creation naturally into their thinking. He knew that this was the beginning of real wisdom, and perhaps it was the start of exciting science careers for both of them.

The spacecraft skimmed by Pluto, picking up some of its gravitational pull to slingshot its way back home to Earth.

Showing the shuttle four billion miles from the earth setting its course around Pluto and back to Earth.

The three of them listened to the next announcement over the intercom with mixed emotions: "Our mission is over and we're homeward bound!" announced Captain Brock.

"All hands secure the ship and prepare to enter **warp speed mode**," ordered Major Paul.

The astronauts were glad to be going home, but they knew they probably never again would have as interesting and exciting an adventure as they had just been on, and they were both sad and happy, as they sat together, and yet alone, with their thoughts.

Questions

1. Describe the atmospheric gases on planet Pluto. What could creationists say about this atmosphere?
2. Where did Pluto get its name?
3. What is the surface temperature of planet Pluto?
4. What is the name of Pluto's moon? Why is this moon so important?

Chapter **22**

HOMEWARD BOUND!

All too soon, the shuttle was zooming home. Much study would follow back on Earth—study involving the rock samples from Mars, thousands of photos, and many, many facts of recorded instrument data.

Ann and Jonathan knew that some day they would be traveling to cities around the world to lecture to students; they would *never* forget this *Voyage to the Planets*.

Their journey back to the earth gave the young people much time to talk to the captain about their analysis of the planets in comparison to planet Earth.

"Captain," Ann addressed him, "you challenged us to look at all the data objectively. You also said that you want us to look at these data from a creationist point of view.

"Well, Jonathan and I were discussing this one time, and we've come to the conclusion that the scientific evidence we've seen demands a Creator."

Jonathan picked up the conversation at this point.

"Captain, we've seen that there isn't one planet suitable for life except planet Earth. In fact, when we look at the planets' orbits and the orbits of their moons, we see the fingerprints of a Creator God. Some moons orbit their planets in opposite directions, and some planets rotate oppositely. Why, there are even sulfuric acids, methane, ammonia, and many other gases that would destroy life. Some of the planets aren't anything but balls of gas.

"When we look at Saturn's orbiting moons, alone, we see things that defy the theory of an accidental, evolutionary origin."

"Yes," observed Ann. "It seems as though someone placed them in the universe precisely for us to see. Everything about this points to a Creator putting them in space. There seems to be no evolutionary theory that could even remotely stand up to what we saw."

The captain spoke up with a serious expression on his face. "I certainly agree with you both. In fact, I think you're on to something. I've been personally evaluating the uniqueness of planet Earth. Our planet is so special it defies description. It's just the right distance from the sun, and it has just the right atmosphere, with about 21 percent oxygen. If it had much more oxygen, the air would be in danger of burning, and if it had much less, it would be difficult for us to breathe. Earth has about 78 percent nitrogen, which is non-combustible, and also just enough carbon dioxide in our atmosphere to keep us warm. If we had too much, it would be too hot for much of life. It could even melt the ice cap, and this would be disastrous. Even so, carbon dioxide is very necessary for plant life and for our general food supply.

"So, overall, I have to agree, and gladly, that the evidence demands a Creator."

"I think you said that if we should see evidence of **symmetry** or **order**, **purpose**, and **interdependence**, this evidence would be irrefutable," said Ann. "I think we've seen **order** and preciseness in the solar system, and we clearly have seen **purpose** in the creation of the earth."

"And we can make a good case for **interdependence** when we see how the sun holds the solar system together," Jonathan added.

Just about that time the familiar voice of Major Paul came over the intercom, and, after all this time, they knew what he was going to say. Securing the ship was routine by now.

The young astronauts braced themselves for entry into the earth's atmosphere.

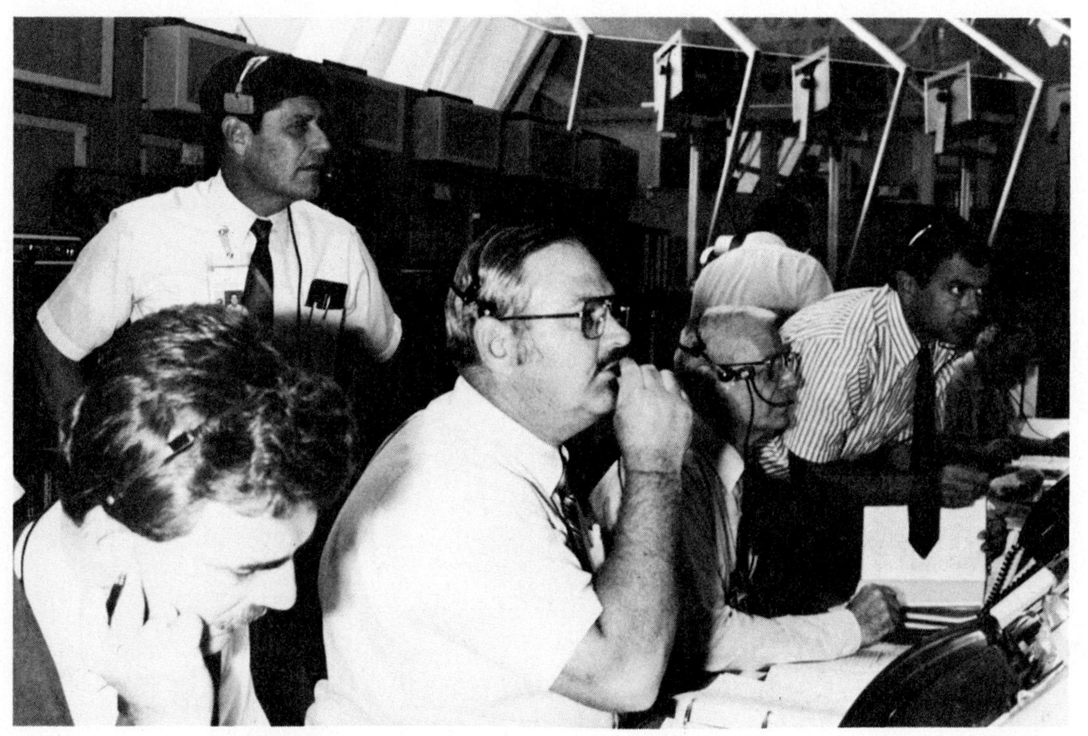

NASA

Questions

1. Give what you think is the best case for creation in all that we've studied so far.
2. What would happen to the earth if there was too much carbon dioxide in the atmosphere?
3. What would happen if the earth's atmosphere contained 98% nitrogen instead of 78% nitrogen?
4. What do you think might happen if the earth had 70% oxygen instead of 21%? (Hint: oxygen is flammable.)

As the astronauts approach the earth's atmosphere, they can see the distinctive uniqueness of planet Earth. (NASA)

Chapter **23**

Hello Again, Planet Earth!

"Look Jonathan," spoke Ann excitedly. "There it is! Of all the planets we've visited, have you ever seen one more beautiful?"

"No," answered Jonathan with a smile. "There's no place like home! And it certainly makes me more aware than ever of the great Creator we worship."

The approach to Edwards Air Force Base was right on target! Once again Major Paul and Captain Brock had teamed up for a flawless landing! They all stayed in the spacecraft for a time so their bodies could adjust to the earth's gravity. They had been gone for a long time in a weightless surrounding, and now they were back at sea level, experiencing the earth's gravity.

The three of them, who had been so close and who had shared so many exciting and wonderful things on this adventure, stopped for a moment to thank their great Creator for allowing them to see His handiwork on this adventure.

"Well," Captain Venture smiled at them, "do you think it was worthwhile?"

"Oh, you know the answer to that, Captain. We're ready to go with you again at a moment's notice," agreed both Ann and Jonathan.

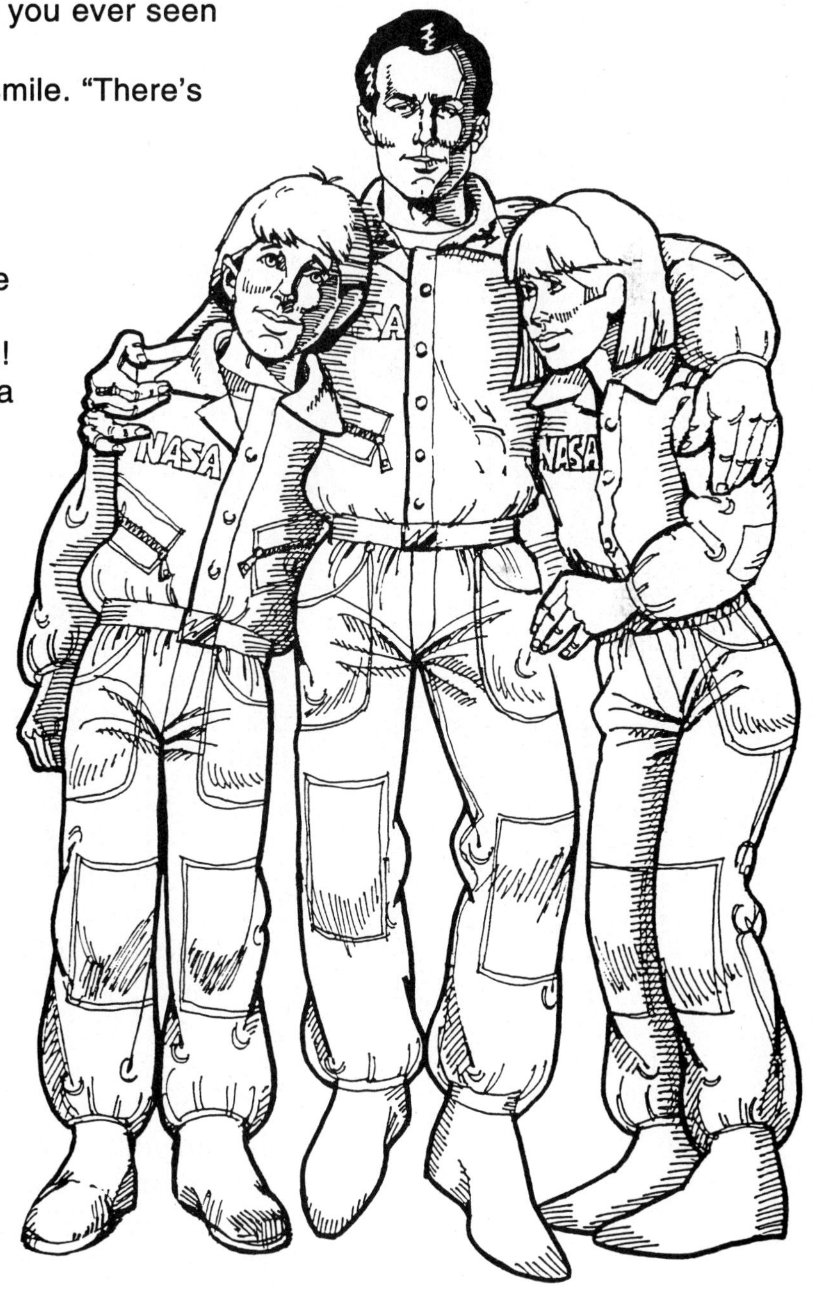

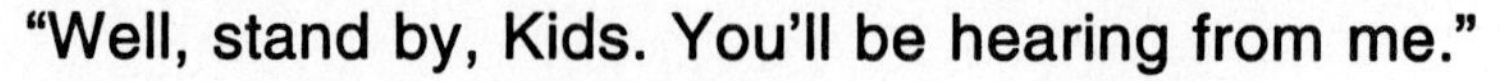

"Well, stand by, Kids. You'll be hearing from me."

They all waved and parted; the young people heading for their rooms and the captain for his debriefing session.

Alone at last in his office, Captain Venture sat down at his desk and opened his Bible. His mind drifted to the awesome nature of the universe, and, particularly, the solar system. He couldn't help but think of Psalm 8:3 and turned to it to read and ponder again:

"When I consider thy heavens, the work of thy fingers, the moon and the stars, which thou hast ordained; what is man, that thou art mindful of him? and the son of man, that thou visitest him?"

The captain smiled to himself. What wonderful, wonderful kids! And what a wonderful, wonderful Creator!

He had been relaxing with his feet on his desk. Suddenly his feet slammed to the floor with a bang, and he hurriedly got up and reached for his jacket.

"Oh, my!" he said to himself. "I've got a chocolate cake and some cream puffs to buy!"

WHAT NEW HORIZONS ARE WAITING FOR US AS WE EXPLORE THIS VAST CREATION GOD HAS MADE FOR MANKIND...
NASA

GLOSSARY

Aphelion
The maximum distance of a planet from the sun.

Apparent Magnitude
The brightness of a space object as seen with the unaided eye. A magnitude of 1 is very bright; 6 is just barely visible.

Asteroid
A "minor planet," smaller than the usual planet-size, which orbits the sun. Most asteroids are located between the orbits of Mars and Jupiter.

Asteroid belt
A belt of asteroids found concentrated beyond the orbit of Mars. These are objects that range in size from 950 km. in diameter to boulder size.

Astronaut
A person trained to travel in space.

Astronomical Unit (AU)
The average earth-sun distance, 93 million miles.

Astronomy
The science dealing with the universe and its parts.

Atmosphere
The envelope of air around the earth.

Atmospheric Pressure
A measure of the weight of air surrounding a planet.

Aurora
The northern and southern lights, caused by solar radiation hitting the earth's atmosphere.

Comet
A mountain-size chunk of frozen matter which orbits the sun. Its orbit alternately brings the comet close to the sun, then to the outer regions of the solar system. When close to the sun, the comet partially melts and develops a

surrounding cloud of vapor and a tail. More than 200 different comets have been identified.

Conjunction

When two objects, such as the sun and a planet, appear in the same part of the sky.

Constellation

A particular group of stars, making up an imaginative picture.

Convection Current

The flow of heat by the upward movement of warm liquid or gas.

Creation

The supernatural origin of life and matter, brought forth by the Word of God. Also applies to the present-day universe.

Density

An object's mass divided by its volume. Density measures the heaviness of matter.

Doppler analysis

Analysis (often done with sound) that depends upon waves or particles moving away from or moving toward an object.

Dosimeter

A film-badge that records exposure to radiation.

Eccentricity

A measure of how elliptical or non-circular an orbital path is.

Ecliptic

The plane of the solar system. The path followed by the sun, moon, and planets across the sky.

Ellipse

The path shape of all orbiting satellites, including planets.

Escape Velocity

The velocity an object needs to escape the gravity pull of a moon or planet. For Earth, the speed is about 25,000 miles per hour.

Favorable opposition
Unusually close position of Mars when opposition occurs near Martian perihelion.

Flyby
A space flight that passes close to a planet or moon, without landing.

Galilean Satellites
The four major moons of Jupiter, discovered by Galileo.

Giant Planets
Jupiter, Saturn, Uranus, and Neptune. They are also called “gas giants,” due to their composition.

Gravity
A fundamental force of nature that results in the attraction of objects. The moon is held captive in its orbit by Earth’s gravity.

Great Red Spot
A giant region of swirling gas on Jupiter’s surface.

Greenhouse Effect
Atmospheric absorption and retention of solar radiation. As a result, the earth warms.

Hubble Space Telescope
A large reflecting telescope placed in Earth orbit in 1989.

Infrared photography
Photography done exclusively with infrared light.

Infrared Radiation
A form of light with an energy slightly less than the visible colors, and with a longer wavelength.

Jovian planets
Giant planets—Jupiter, Saturn, Neptune, Uranus.

Kepler’s Laws
Rules that explain planet orbits, speeds, and planet distances from the sun.

Lander
A component of a space probe designed to land on the surface of a moon or planet.

Light year

The distance that light travels through space in a year, moving at 186,000 miles per second. A light year is nearly six trillion miles.

Magnetometer

An instrument that measures the strength and direction of a magnetic field.

Magnitude

A measure of the brightness of an object in space.

Mass

A measure of an object's total amount of matter.

Mean distance:

A middle point (the average) between two extremes.

Military time

Time is expressed between 0-2400 hours. As examples, 7 a.m. is 0700 hours, noon is 1200 hours, 6 p.m. is 1800 hours, and midnight is 2400 hours.

Moon

All natural objects that revolve around planets.

NASA

An acronym for the National Aeronautics and Space Administration. This agency directs the U.S. space program.

Opposition

The position of an outer planet when it is opposite the sun as seen from the earth.

Orbit

The path of the moon as it circles a planet, or the path of a planet around the sun.

Perihelion

The minimum distance of a planet from the sun.

Planet

A large object (usually greater than 1000 miles in diameter) which circles a star. Nine known planets orbit the sun. They have no light of their own, but reflect the sunlight.

Planetarium
A projection device for studying stars and planets in a dome.

Radiation
An invisible stream of subatomic particles or waves, often with high energy.

Retro slowdown
Slowing down the rocket ship with its astro-rockets.

Retrograde motion
Either the backward rotation of a planet, or its apparent backward wandering through the stars.

Revolution
Orbital motion of one object around another. The earth revolves around the sun once each year.

Rotation
The spinning of an object about its own axis. The earth rotates once every twenty-four hours.

Satellite
A natural or man-made object that orbits a larger object. The space shuttle and the moon are satellites of the earth. In turn, the earth is a satellite of the sun.

Solar System
The sun and the surrounding group of objects which orbit the sun, including planets, asteroids, and comets.

Spectroanalyzer (Spectrograph)
An instrument that identifies particular elements in a sample of matter.

Spectrum
A band of colors like that in a rainbow, produced when light is divided into its various color components.

Sun
Our closest star. The center of the solar system.

Terrestrial Planets
Mercury, Venus, Earth, and Mars. They are also called "inner planets."

Ultraviolet Radiation

A form of light with an energy level slightly greater than the visible colors, and having a shorter wavelength.

Van Allen Radiation Belts

Regions surrounding the earth where space radiation is trapped by the earth's magnetic field.

Velocity

A measure of the speed and direction of an object. The distance traveled by an object in a certain time period, divided by the time.

Warp speed

A fictitious speed faster than the speed of light.

BIBLIOGRAPHY

Bliss, Richard. 1991. *Voyage to the Stars.* ICR. San Diego. Explores the stars beyond the planets.

DeYoung, Don. 1989. *Astronomy and the Bible.* Baker Book House. Grand Rapids. Contains 100 basic astronomy questions and answers from a creation perspective.

Ferris, Timothy. 1988. *Coming of Age in the Milky Way.* William Morrow and Co., Inc. New York. The history of astronomy, including the solar system.

Journey into the universe through time and space. A chart supplement to the *National Geographic.* June 1983. p. 704a. vol. 163, no. 6. National Geographic Society, Washington D.C. Excellent drawings of the solar system, Milky Way galaxy, and the universe.

Kuhn, Karl F. 1994. *In Quest of the Universe.* West Publishing Co., New York. A college text with excellent data pages about the planets.

Menzel, Donald and Pasachoff, Jay. *A Field Guide to Stars and Planets*, 2nd ed. (Sponsored by National Audubon Society.) Houghton Mifflin Co. Boston. 1983.

Baker, David. *The Henry Holt Guide to Astronomy.* Henry Holt and Company. N.Y. 1978.

Moore, Patrick. *New Concise Atlas of the Universe.* Rand McNally and Company. New York. Chicago. San Francisco. 1978.

Yeates, C.M., Johnson, T.V. *Galileo Exploration of Jupiter's System.* NASA. 1985.

Information Summaries. *Our Solar System at a Glance.* NASA. 1991.

Remembered Images. NASA. 1958–83.

S.E.T.I. NASA. 1990

V.A.R.S. NASA. 1989.

Muirdenm, James. The Universe. *The Simon and Schuster Illustrated Encyclopedia*. 1978.

Flight. How things work. Time Life Books. 1990.

Science Discoveries from the space program. A Meeting with the Universe. NASA. 1981.

NASA, the First 25 years. 1958–1983.

Voyage through the Universe. The Near Planets. Time Life. 1989.

Voyage through the Universe. The Far Planets. Time Life. 1990.

Voyage through the Universe. Life Search. Time Life. 1988.

Voyage through the Universe. The Third Planet. Time Life. 1989.

Voyage through the Universe. Outbound. Time Life. 1989.